THE **FORTUNES** OF **TEXAS**

SHIPMENT 1

Healing Dr. Fortune by Judy Duarte
Mendoza's Return by Susan Crosby
Fortune's Just Desserts by Marie Ferrarella
Fortune's Secret Baby by Christyne Butler
Fortune Found by Victoria Pade
Fortune's Cinderella by Karen Templeton

SHIPMENT 2

Fortune's Valentine Bride by Marie Ferrarella
Mendoza's Miracle by Judy Duarte
Fortune's Hero by Susan Crosby
Fortune's Unexpected Groom by Nancy Robards Thompson
Fortune's Perfect Match by Allison Leigh
Her New Year's Fortune by Allison Leigh

SHIPMENT 3

A Date with Fortune by Susan Crosby
A Small Fortune by Marie Ferrarella
Marry Me, Mendoza! by Judy Duarte
Expecting Fortune's Heir by Cindy Kirk
A Change of Fortune by Crystal Green
Happy New Year, Baby Fortune! by Leanne Banks
A Sweetheart for Jude Fortune by Cindy Kirk

SHIPMENT 4

Lassoed by Fortune by Marie Ferrarella
A House Full of Fortunes! by Judy Duarte
Falling for Fortune by Nancy Robards Thompson
Fortune's Prince by Allison Leigh
A Royal Fortune by Judy Duarte
Fortune's Little Heartbreaker by Cindy Kirk

SHIPMENT 5

Mendoza's Secret Fortune by Marie Ferrarella
The Taming of Delaney Fortune by Michelle Major
My Fair Fortune by Nancy Robards Thompson
Fortune's June Bride by Allison Leigh
Plain Jane and the Playboy by Marie Ferrarella
Valentine's Fortune by Allison Leigh

SHIPMENT 6

Triple Trouble by Lois Faye Dyer
Fortune's Woman by RaeAnne Thayne
A Fortune Wedding by Kristin Hardy
Her Good Fortune by Marie Ferrarella
A Tycoon in Texas by Crystal Green
In a Texas Minute by Stella Bagwell

SHIPMENT 7

Cowboy at Midnight by Ann Major
A Baby Changes Everything by Marie Ferrarella
In the Arms of the Law by Peggy Moreland
Lone Star Rancher by Laurie Paige
The Good Doctor by Karen Rose Smith
The Debutante by Elizabeth Bevarly

SHIPMENT 8

Keeping Her Safe by Myrna Mackenzie
The Law of Attraction by Kristi Gold
Once a Rebel by Sheri WhiteFeather
Military Man by Marie Ferrarella
Fortune's Legacy by Maureen Child
The Reckoning by Christie Ridgway

THE FORTUNES OF TEXAS

THE GOOD DOCTOR

USA TODAY BESTSELLING AUTHOR

Karen Rose Smith

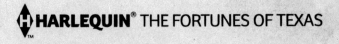

HARLEQUIN® THE FORTUNES OF TEXAS

Special thanks and acknowledgment are given to
Karen Rose Smith for her contribution to
the Fortunes of Texas: Reunion continuity.

ISBN-13: 978-1-335-68075-4

Recycling programs
for this product may
not exist in your area.

The Good Doctor

Printed in U.S.A.

www.Harlequin.com

USA TODAY bestselling author **Karen Rose Smith** has written over ninety novels. Her passion is caring for her four rescued cats, and her hobbies are gardening, cooking and photography. An only child, Karen delved into books at an early age. Even though she escaped into story worlds, she had many cousins around her on weekends. Families are a strong theme in her novels. Find out more about Karen at karenrosesmith.com.

To my agent, Evan Marshall. Thank you for your ongoing support, encouragement and counsel.

Many thanks to Dr. Steve Goldberg and his wife, Kristi, for their help with medical research. The information you provided was invaluable.

Chapter 1

"You've got it all now," Linda Clark decided as she appraised her brother.

"Just wait till those nurses get a gander at you," Stacey agreed, her smile as wide as her sister's.

Dr. Peter Clark swiftly closed his office door, hoping no one had heard. "Cool it, you two," he demanded in a stern voice as he strode to his desk, wondering how long this visit was going to last. He had an appointment in fifteen minutes. His sisters weren't in awe of him as some of his patients were, so it might be hard to kick them out. He loved them dearly but sometimes…

"I don't know why I let you dress me like a mannequin," he grumbled. He was still not sure the navy tweed blazer was something he would have chosen on his own. He definitely wouldn't have bought the silk shirt and the patterned designer tie.

"You turned thirty-nine yesterday, and you wouldn't even let us give you a party. The least we could do is spruce you up a bit," Linda teased, brushing her dark brown hair away from her face. "Now tall, dark and handsome really applies. I like the new haircut, and we didn't even have anything to do with *that*."

"My regular barber was out of town."

A laugh came from Stacey's direction. "Thank goodness! The only thing we could add now is color contacts to make your eyes a little greener."

He'd had enough. They'd taken him to lunch and then accompanied him to a men's store to pick up his tuxedo for Friday night. Despite his protests, they'd insisted on buying him a blazer, shirt and tie as birthday gifts, convincing the store manager to have them pressed so he could wear the outfit back to the office. His usual routine wasn't as frivolous, not by a long shot. Most days he was in the hospital or in surgery from dawn to dusk. This venture into the lighter side of life just didn't fit him any more than some of those blazers he'd tried on.

He deliberately checked his watch. "I have an appointment in ten minutes."

"We're not leaving until you assure us you'll show up on Friday night."

Counting to five, he tried to keep the impatience from his voice. "You talked me into the bachelor auction because it's for a good cause. I never go back on my word. Not even if that means I have to endure the humiliation of standing on a runway and having women bid on me. Now, as I said…"

Linda sighed. "Your life is much too serious. I couldn't stand doing what you do. A pediatric neurosurgeon holds too much power in his hands. How do you handle that responsibility?"

"Very carefully," he replied seriously.

Nothing meant more to him than his work and the kids he treated. In fact there was one right now who was breaking his heart. The bachelor auction would be raising money for high-tech equipment for the pediatrics wing to help children like Celeste. That was the only reason he'd agreed to be a part of it. That, and the fact that the wing had been built as a memorial to his mother. If only there was someone like his mom to help with his little patient.

She needed loving care as much as she needed high-tech equipment and surgery—maybe even more.

There was a knock on his office door and Katrina, his receptionist, poked her head inside. His office would be chaos without her. He was in partnership with two other neurosurgeons and she made sure the organization of their schedules and appointments didn't interfere with the work they did. She was a petite dynamo in her forties with short-cropped, curly black hair, a round face and an impish smile.

"Dr. Violet Fortune is here. I didn't think you'd want to keep her waiting."

Linda's brows arched under her dark bangs. Stacey's mouth rounded as she digested the Fortune name.

"A Fortune coming to see you? What's all that about?" Linda asked. Then, as if a lightbulb went on in her head, she snapped her fingers. "Oh, I get it. Violet Fortune's a neurologist with a reputation almost as good as yours. Maybe she came all the way from New York to consult with you."

"Okay," Peter said, rising to his feet. "You did *not* hear a name. You have amnesia about anything Katrina said."

"We'll see Violet Fortune on our way out.

Her picture has been in the *Red Rock Gazette* now and then," Linda concluded. "You know, that paper *you* never read because medical journals are more important."

His sisters were successful women in their own right. Stacey owned a small boutique in one of San Antonio's gallerias, and Linda was a loan officer with a major financial institution. Both of them, however, seemed to be able to see the lighter side of life much better than he could. Maybe because he'd been the firstborn. Maybe because when their mother had died, the event had shaken his world the most. Perhaps that was why they'd been able to accept his father's quick remarriage afterward—as well as their stepmother—and he never could.

Both of them were on their feet now, realizing he did have work to do. Linda gave him a quick hug. "Happy day-after-your-birthday once more." She patted the sleeve of his blazer. "Really hot," she kidded again.

He couldn't help but laugh then as Stacey hugged him, too, and added, "If not before, we'll see you Friday night. Just make sure that black tie's straight before you stroll down the runway, okay?"

When his sisters stepped into the hall, he decided to walk them out. He didn't want them waylaying Dr. Fortune out of curiosity. They must have sensed that because they grinned at him, waved and cast a few long glances at the woman sitting in his waiting room. Seconds later they were gone and he turned his attention to Violet Fortune.

As soon as he did, he was caught off guard. She was stunning. Absolutely stunning. Her reputation as a brilliant diagnostician had already reached Texas. At only thirty-three, she'd already made her mark in her field. Maybe he'd envisioned her in a lab coat, with a severe hairdo and a no-nonsense demeanor, but the flesh-and-blood Violet Fortune was the polar opposite.

Her hair was light brown with sun streaks, chin-length and had obviously been cut and styled by someone who knew what he was doing. It was silky and bouncy, complementing the patrician lines of her face. Her eyes were light blue, sparkling and vulnerable. That surprised him, too, but then he didn't know why she was here. Certainly she knew he had a pediatric neurosurgery practice. Did she have a child? Had his friends Ryan and Lily Fortune recommended him?

"Dr. Fortune?" he asked, just to make sure.

Standing, placing the magazine she'd been

paging through on the chair beside her, she gave him a smile that socked him in the solar plexus. "Yes, I'm Dr. Fortune. Are you Dr. Clark?"

"Last time I looked," he countered with his own smile, ignoring the lightninglike signals his libido was sending his body.

Since October in Red Rock, Texas, could still be warm, she was wearing a full-skirted royal blue dress with a yellow-and-red design around the hem. He suspected the short, boxy jacket covered straps to a sundress. Dark red high heels showed the curves of her legs to perfection, he noticed, then he quickly jerked his gaze up to hers.

When he extended his hand, the action helped him focus and he could more easily ignore the reaction he was having to her. "It's good to meet you, although I'm a bit puzzled as to why you're here."

"Ryan and Lily have spoken highly of you."

The soft grip of her hand registered along with everything else about her. She seemed to be looking into his eyes with the same intensity he was looking into hers, and that created electricity.

"I think highly of them," he said, releasing her hand and pulling away.

Breaking eye contact, she quickly glanced

around the office but no one else was in the room. Despite the fact his receptionist was behind her glass window, still Violet kept her voice low. "This visit has to do with Ryan."

All business now, hearing the somberness in her voice, he motioned down the hall. "Let's talk in my office."

Having decided long ago not to follow in any man's footsteps, Violet kept up with Peter's long strides, studying him while he didn't have his attention on her, wondering why the earth had seemed to shake a little when he'd taken her hand in his. She didn't react that way to men, especially not male doctors. In fact, she'd begun to think something was wrong with her—that she was frigid. Since her teenage years when she'd so desperately sought a boy's attention, something in her heart had simply turned off when it came to romantic relationships. Peter's tall, lean but muscular physique, his short but thick black hair and his piercing green eyes had created a twitter inside of her she couldn't seem to still.

His office door was open, and he stood aside so she could enter before him. A gentleman, she thought. Wasn't that rare? She'd grown up with four brothers who treated her as a projection of themselves. Chivalry had never been part of their relationship, though the brothers were fiercely protective of her.

The aroma of coffee wafted around the office and Peter gestured to the pot on the credenza that had obviously just been brewed. "Katrina must have snuck in here and started that for me. Would you like a cup?"

"No thanks. I'm fine." Violet was worried and anxious enough. She didn't need caffeine revving her up more. Maybe that was why she felt this attraction to Dr. Clark, because her guard was down. It had been down for over two months now. That was why she'd come to Texas to her brothers' ranch.

Apparently deciding his own mug of coffee could wait, Peter Clark lowered himself into the high-back, leather swivel chair behind his desk. He waited until she'd seated herself in one of the gray tweed chairs across from it. The barrier and the bit of distance made her feel more self-possessed than when he'd greeted her in the reception area.

"So what can I do for you?" he asked, curiosity evident in his expression.

Taking her dark red clutch bag in her hands, she opened it and extracted a legal-sized envelope. When she handed it to him, she concluded seriously, "You'd better read this first. It's from Ryan."

After he glanced at it, he looked even more perplexed. "Essentially it's a release form giving you permission to discuss him with me."

She nodded. "That's precisely what it is. I'm not only a relative and good friend to Ryan and Lily, but I'm a neurologist, as well."

"I know that. I'm familiar with the articles you've published. You've made a name for yourself in a short amount of time."

"I guess New York isn't as far from Texas as I sometimes think it is."

"The world *is* getting smaller, but it's more than that. Red Rock is a small community and the Fortune name means something here. Besides your relationship to Ryan and Lily, your brothers have established themselves, too."

Her brothers Jack, Steven, Miles and Clyde had vacationed in Red Rock as kids and they all had decided to settle here as adults. Steven and his new bride, Amy, had bought his own ranch, Loma Vista, and was renovating it. A gala, during which the governor was going to present Ryan with an award, would take place there next month. Miles and Clyde's cattle and chicken ranch, the Flying Aces, where she was staying, was thriving. Her oldest brother, Jack, had just married recently and settled here, too.

"What I'm getting at," Peter continued, "is that the Fortunes are continuously discussed in Red Rock, and that includes you."

"Me? I don't even live here."

"No, but your name and career are bandied about along with all the other Fortunes. Most people in town know your history."

"What history would that be?"

"Education history for one thing. I heard with tutors you graduated high school a year early. You also did a four-year college program in three. In med school, you earned respect quickly and began seeing patients in New York City when you joined a prestigious neurological practice there. Your life's an open book," he added with some amusement.

An open book? Not by a long shot. No one but her immediate family knew why her parents had hired a private tutor for her and why she'd concentrated so hard on her studies. Not even Ryan and Lily knew what had happened to her as a teenager, the wrong decisions she'd made and the foolish choices.

Rerouting the conversation back to her visit, she nodded to the letter in Peter's hand. "I'm here because Ryan asked me to speak to you."

"About?"

"He's having symptoms."

"What kind of symptoms?"

She took another paper from her purse, opened it and laid it on his desk. "First of all, I need to tell you that Lily knows nothing about this and that's the way Ryan wants it. That's also why he took me aside at Steven and Amy's wedding to talk to me privately. He'd begun having severe headaches and he didn't want to consult with a doctor in Red Rock or San Antonio because he'd tried to brush off the pain at first. He also didn't want any more rumors to get started. There have been enough about him concerning…everything."

"He's not still a suspect in the Christopher Jamison murder, is he? The police certainly should have ruled him out by now."

It sounded as if Peter had no doubts about Ryan's innocence. "Apparently they *haven't* ruled him out. That stress alone could cause headaches. But he told me he'd never had this type of headache before, so I took him seriously."

"Are you staying at the Double Crown?"

"No, I'm staying with Miles at the Flying Aces while Clyde and my new sister-in-law Jessica are on their honeymoon. Miles insisted I stay there so we can visit. I can't show too much concern about Ryan because Lily and everyone else will become suspicious."

Peter took the evaluation form she handed him and looked it over. His expression became more somber as he did. "He's having some tingling in his arm?"

"Yes."

"You said he didn't want to see anyone local. Why come to me when my speciality is pediatric neurosurgery?"

"He trusts you, Dr. Clark. You'll keep all this confidential, including my involvement. I've recommended he have testing done but I'm not licensed to practice in Texas and I don't have hospital privileges here. You, however, do. Ryan thought if the two of us worked together, we could get to the bottom of whatever is wrong. It would safeguard his privacy."

After a second look at the report she'd written, Peter's gaze met hers. "I want to talk to Ryan myself."

"He'd rather not come here, and he doesn't want Lily or anyone else in the family to know."

When Peter rubbed his chin thoughtfully, Violet couldn't help but notice what a definitive jawline he had, what large strong-looking hands. "All right. I'm glad Ryan believes he can trust me. We can meet at my house. I can examine him and then we can decide what to do next."

"When are you available?" Violet asked.

"Tonight."

Obviously Peter Clark didn't like Ryan's symptoms any more than she did. "I'll call Ryan and see if he's free."

She took her little blue cell phone from her purse. A few minutes later, after a brief conversation with Ryan in which they all agreed on a time, she closed the phone and dropped it back into her handbag.

"Ryan said to make sure to tell you he'll pay you double your usual fee because he knows this is an inconvenience."

"Ryan's a friend. There won't be a fee, not for tonight."

"He won't like that."

Peter smiled. "Maybe not, but it will be my only condition for examining him."

"I can see why he respects you," she said softly.

Silent communication passed between them and because of their concern for Ryan, a bond was formed. However, that bond seemed to be more personal than professional.

Standing, she met his gaze. "It was good to

meet you, Dr. Clark. I don't want to take up any more of your time."

"It's Peter," he corrected her.

"Peter," she murmured.

Holding her gaze, he seemed to be waiting for something. Finally, with a wry smile turning up the corners of his lips, he asked, "And should I call you Dr. Fortune or Violet?"

She felt her cheeks turn hot and couldn't remember the last time she'd blushed. "Violet's fine," she decided, feeling much too warm in the small office.

When he rose to his feet and came around the desk, they were standing very close. "Ryan is lucky to have you in the family."

"He and my dad have always been close. I grew up respecting him, and he's like a favorite uncle. I don't want anything to happen to him."

"This could be serious."

She already knew that, the possibilities having kept her awake the past few nights. Still, she realized Peter felt he had to put the probability into words, so that she could take it as a warning, so that she wouldn't deny what might be the cause of Ryan's problems. "I know this could be serious. But on the other hand, stress and tension could cause symptoms, too."

"That's possible. We'll proceed one step at a time."

Feeling as if she could stand there all day just looking at Peter, absorbing his strength, his concern and his compassion, she gave herself a mental shake. She didn't need any of those things from him. Ryan did.

With a deep breath, she stepped away from Peter's powerful aura and walked toward the door. "You don't have to see me out. Ryan says he knows where your house is located, so I guess I'll see you tonight."

"Tonight," Peter agreed, his deep voice making the word sound like a commitment.

As Violet escaped into the hall and closed the office door behind her, she knew Dr. Peter Clark's commitment was to Ryan Fortune.

"That's the one—number seven-seventeen." Ryan directed Violet to Peter Clark's house on the western outskirts of Red Rock.

Developments were springing up randomly in the small community, and it was getting larger. When Violet was growing up and her family visited Ryan and his family on the Double Crown, she loved their little excursions into Red Rock with its rural fields, its round park-like town square with the white gazebo, its ice-cream parlor and family restaurants. Not that Violet had ever wanted to live here. She loved New York City and that was her home.

"I can't believe all these houses just sprang up over the last year," Ryan grumbled. "Pretty soon Red Rock's going to stretch out and meet San Antonio."

Red Rock was a twenty-mile drive from San Antonio. "I don't think you have to worry about that quite yet."

"The garage door's going up. Peter must have been watching for us."

Peter Clark's house was a country-ranch style and angled across the lot in an upside-down open V.

"Looks like a lot of house for a bachelor," Ryan commented as she pulled into the garage next to an SUV.

A light was on in the garage and Peter stood in the doorway leading into the house. Dressed in khaki slacks and a black polo shirt, he looked taller and more broad-shouldered than he had this afternoon. The sight of him seemed to make Violet's pulse race faster, but she told herself she was just anxious about Ryan. Deep down, though, she was eager to know more about Peter—too eager. For all she knew, he might be involved with someone. For all she knew, he might have moved into this new house in order to share his life with his significant other.

Sharing her life with someone had never come close to competing with her career.

Her career.

The Washburn case had shaken her confidence more than anything else ever had. She'd taken a cruise to try to gain perspective on what had happened. That hadn't helped. So since she was coming to Red Rock for her brother's wedding, she'd cleared her schedule for a few more weeks to try to get her head on straight again.

She didn't need a sexy neurosurgeon making it spin. In a few weeks she'd be returning to her practice in New York. There was no doubt about that, and no room in her life for an emotional entanglement that would only hurt her when it had to end.

"Are you ready?" she asked Ryan, noticing he hadn't unfastened his seat belt.

"No, I'm *not* ready. But let's get this over with anyway."

After they exited the car, Peter's smile was congenial as he held his hand out to Ryan. "It's good to see you again."

Dressed in boots, jeans and a green plaid, snap-button shirt, Ryan was solidly built from years of ranch work. He was still darkly handsome at age fifty-nine, deeply tanned from riding and working under the Texas sun. Violet admired his good heart as much as his accomplishments on the Double Crown and at Fortune TX, Ltd., where he acted as an advisor and sat on the board of directors.

The doorway from the garage led past the mudroom into a large living room. Violet noticed an expansive deck that seemed to go on forever outside of the living room's sliding glass doors.

"Interesting place you've got here," she remarked as they walked into the kitchen and stood peering into the great room with its cathedral ceiling and immense fan.

Sliding glass doors from that room also led out onto the deck, and Violet glimpsed a hot tub. The fireplace in the great room was fashioned of beautiful gray stone. A mission-style sofa and chair were grouped around it, their cushions woven with fabric striped in gray, tan and black. The living room had been equipped with an entertainment center, large TV and contemporary glass tables. In that room, the decor was an extension of the outdoors with earth tones and rustic textures. It still looked a bit empty.

"I really like the design of this house," she said with admiration.

"It's different," Peter agreed. "And it suits me. I'm not here often enough to enjoy it, though. If I don't soon put something on the walls, my sisters are threatening to do it for me."

"You come from a large family?" Violet asked.

"Two biological sisters. My parents took in a lot of foster kids, and they feel like brothers and sisters, too."

Peter's gaze passed over Violet's light blue, short-sleeved blouse and indigo jeans. She felt herself get very warm. She'd been tempted to wear something less casual but had told herself what she wore was simply not important.

"Would you like something to drink?" Peter asked.

Ryan shook his head. "I don't want to tie you up too long."

"All right. Violet, if you're interested, help yourself to anything in the refrigerator." He motioned to a hall that led to the other side of the house. "My study's down this way. Let's go in there."

Then the men disappeared and Violet was left standing in the center of Peter Clark's house all alone.

She couldn't help snooping a bit. Well, not snooping, but absorbing Peter's surroundings.

Her apartment was cluttered with mementoes from her childhood—presents her brothers and her parents had given her and selected items that simply carried memories. Now as she wandered toward a pine cabinet with glass doors, she peeked through the glass. There was a picture in a silver frame of a woman dressed in bell-bottomed slacks standing with a man who looked very much like Peter. Beside it stood three leather-bound books that were classics, a photograph of the same woman, older now, standing with five children. On another shelf, Violet spotted a duck decoy carved from wood and intricately painted, a Kachina and a wicker basket filled with seashells. There were several arrowheads and a picture of two young women. Peter's sisters?

Glancing toward the study, she realized she was taking inventory to keep her mind off what was happening in there. Would Peter's findings be different from hers?

A half hour later, Violet was staring out into Peter's backyard unseeingly when Ryan and the neurosurgeon emerged from the study.

Ryan raked his hand through his hair. "He

made me do all the same things you did and asked a heck of a lot of questions."

"I think Ryan needs an MRI," Peter advised calmly. "I'll call a colleague of mine in Houston, where I did my residency, and see if he can set it up there."

"But *you'll* be my doctor?" Ryan asked hopefully.

"My speciality is children, Ryan, but let's not jump ahead of ourselves. We'll do the test and then go from there."

"You're right. That sounds reasonable." He looked from Peter to Violet. "I know you two probably want to talk about me. I'll just go on outside and take a look around."

As if knowing neither of them would argue with him, he unlatched the sliding glass doors and stepped outside.

After Ryan had closed the door and walked farther out onto the deck, Violet asked, "Do you think his condition is serious?"

"At this stage, there's no way of knowing. The MRI will tell us what comes next."

"Is there any reason why Ryan shouldn't drive? I convinced him to let me bring him tonight, but he's not the type of man who likes to be chauffeured."

"I asked him about blackouts and he said

he hasn't had any. He insists he hasn't been dizzy, either. So until something other than the headaches develop, I can't tell him he shouldn't drive."

When Violet thought about the possibilities of what could be wrong with Ryan, she felt her chin quiver. Suddenly the idea of losing Ryan was much too real.

Coming closer, Peter studied her for a long moment. "What?"

Feeling embarrassed, she shook her head. "He's...he's more than a patient to me."

A tear escaped the corner of her eye and rolled down her cheek, and she quickly swiped at it.

Reaching out, Peter clasped her shoulder. "Don't borrow trouble."

"I can't help but worry. It hasn't been that long since he and Lily found each other again. They're so happy."

"Yes, they are. But whether this is stress or something more serious, I know she'll support him just as you will...just as I will."

Peter's hand on her shoulder was comforting. It was as if she could feel his strength seeping into her. "You'd never know I deal with life and death and grim diagnoses all the time."

"Grim diagnoses?"

"There just seems to have been a lot of them lately. Before I left New York there were two young women with MS, and a pregnant mother who died—"

She stopped abruptly, not knowing what she was doing. She didn't unload. That simply wasn't her nature. She handled what came her way without leaning on anyone.

"What else?" he asked, his green eyes kind.

"Nothing, really. I don't know what's gotten into me. All I'm doing is riding, catching up on medical journals and visiting with my brother Miles. You'd think I'd be as happy as the proverbial lark."

"Anyone can get burned out."

"Do you?" she asked.

With a wry smile and a half shrug, he answered, "Not yet." Then he became more serious. "But it can sneak up on you."

Gazing into Peter's eyes, Violet couldn't seem to look away. His hand was still resting comfortingly on her shoulder, but the comfort was becoming an awareness that easily could turn into something else.

Self-consciously, she motioned toward the deck. "I'd better tell Ryan I'm ready to go or he'll think we're keeping something from him."

Dropping his hand to his side, Peter agreed.

"Yes, he probably will. I'll call you tomorrow as soon as I talk to my friend in Houston."

"I'm staying in the pool house at the Flying Aces. It doesn't have a phone, but I can give you my cell phone number."

She took a card from her purse and handed it to him. "I've written the number on there."

When he took the card from her, his fingers grazed hers.

Her gaze lifted to his strong profile.

She was acting like a schoolgirl with a crush and that had to stop. Going to the glass doors, she opened them. Ryan hadn't told Lily where he was actually going tonight. In fact, he'd lied to her. He'd told her he was taking Violet to see a horse he was thinking about buying. On their drive home, she was going to convince him to tell his wife what was actually going on.

That way Violet wouldn't think about Peter Clark. That way she could ignore all the sensations she'd always wanted to feel but had never felt before.

She didn't need a man in her life. She did *not*.

Chapter 2

Violet drove up to the main house on the Double Crown Ranch the following morning, parking in front of a garden where sage plants and ornamental grasses grew. She was worried. By nature, she hated lying, even by omission. Yet she owed Ryan confidentiality and couldn't tell Lily where the two of them had been last night. She wished Ryan would tell his wife about his symptoms and that Peter was going to have an MRI arranged.

Peter.

Shaking her head, as if that could rid her thoughts of the neurosurgeon, Violet walked through the arched entryway and opened the wrought-iron gate. A curved stone walkway led through the outer courtyard where native plants and rocks were arranged in a miniature arroyo. Flowering vines perfumed the area as she mounted the steps that led to a wide wooden door in the covered entryway.

At her knock, Rosita Perez opened the door. Pleasantly plump, dressed in a peasant blouse and a long gauzy skirt, she patted her bun as if to make certain it was still there, then smiled.

"You're right on time. Lanie Meyers isn't here yet. Traffic from Austin could be keeping her. But Mr. Ryan and Lily are waiting in the inner courtyard. Come on and I'll get you a cup of coffee."

This brunch had been planned since last week. Next month the governor would be honoring Ryan with his presence at Steven's new ranch. The gala was already being organized. The governor's daughter, Lanie, acting as an emissary for her father, would be coming to brunch to tell Ryan and Lily how glad she was that Ryan was being honored with the Hensley-Robinson Award. It was a preliminary meeting to fill in the Fortunes on some of the arrangements, and Lily had invited Violet to join them.

The foyer of Ryan's ranch house opened up into a great room with a high, beamed ceiling.

As Rosita showed her through the room, Violet asked, "How's Savannah?" Savannah was married to Cruz Perez, Rosita's son. The couple had a five-year-old and were expecting another child soon.

Rosita smiled. "She's doing well now after that premature labor scare. She just has to take it easy, and Cruz is making sure she does that. I help out with Luke whenever I can."

"Tell her I hope to see her soon and that I wish her and Cruz well."

Giving Violet's hand a little squeeze, Rosita nodded, then opened one of the wood-framed glass doors that led into the inner courtyard. Violet loved the area where a fountain bubbled and an old-fashioned swing stood under a vine-covered arbor. Descending the few steps, she headed toward one of the glass-topped tables.

Right away she could feel the tension. Whatever Ryan and Lily had been discussing had put a frown on Lily's face. Had he told his wife he was at Peter Clark's last night?

However, Violet soon knew that wasn't the case because Ryan gave her a barely perceptible shake of his head.

Spotting Violet, Lily quickly replaced her frown with a smile. At fifty-nine, she was still beautiful. Her Apache and Spanish heritage had given her high cheekbones and large dark eyes framed by thick lashes. She had a wonderful figure and wore her hair in a shiny bob a little longer than Violet's own hair. She was wearing white slacks today with a colorful striped sweater.

"I'm so glad you could join us this morning." She gave Violet a hug, which Violet affectionately returned. Always comfortable with Lily, she could usually talk to her easily. That was why it would be so hard to hide anything from her.

Ryan gave Violet a hug, too, as Lily asked, "So how did you like that horse Ryan took you to see last night? He tells me it's a Morgan, brown with a white blaze."

Violet's thoughts seemed jumbled as she tried to come up with an appropriate response. Fortunately, just then, the chime of the doorbell could be heard in the courtyard.

As Rosita hurried away, Lily poured a cup of coffee for Violet from a silver serving set. "That should be the governor's daughter." Forgetting the horse her husband had mentioned, Lily motioned to the coffee. "You take it black with sugar, right?"

"Sure do. Coffee in the lounge at the hospital is usually strong and stale. The sugar helps. I've gotten used to it that way."

Lily motioned Violet to a seat and placed the cup of coffee there. "We are definitely creatures of habit, maybe too much so." Her gaze shot to Ryan.

His mouth tightened and some unspoken message seemed to pass between them.

Hearing footsteps, Violet turned and saw Lanie Myers coming down the steps. She was a beauty and, from what Lily had told her, often in the society pages with her blond hair, blue eyes and voluptuous figure. She had a reputation for being a bit wild, at least that was what the gossip columnists said.

After greetings all around, Lanie joined them at the table.

Ryan asked good naturedly, "How's your father's reelection campaign going?"

"It's going," she observed in a wry tone that made everyone laugh. "Well, it is," she added with a little shrug. "I don't know how he does it, shaking all those hands, trying to please so many people. I just got back from a shopping trip in L.A., so I escaped the fray for a while."

When Violet gave the former debutante an appraisal, she noted Lanie's cream halter dress shouted designer label all the way. "Do you ever fly to New York to shop?"

Lanie took a few sips of the orange juice Rosita had placed before her. "I love New York— not only the shopping, but the shows. I try to get there a few times a year. Lily told me you live there. It must be wonderful to have access to the theater district, the symphony and ballet all the time."

"It is, and I should take advantage of it more. But I don't."

"Violet's a neurologist," Lily interjected. "When she's not tied up with patients, she's writing articles. She also sits on the board for a battered women's shelter."

"You have a terrifically serious life," Lanie mused. "No wonder you don't have much time for the theater."

"Violet's mother, Lacey, has been fighting for worthwhile causes since she was a young woman," Lily explained. "That couldn't help but rub off on Violet."

Lily was right about that, Violet thought. Her mother was still fighting for causes she believed in. When she was growing up, Violet had mistakenly believed that her mom's causes were more important than her family. But she'd been wrong about that. It had taken a crisis to prove to her that both of her parents as well as her brothers valued her more than anything else in their lives. Her experience at fifteen might have made her reticent to become involved in intimate relationships, but it had also made her realize she truly wasn't alone.

Deflecting conversation from *her* life, Violet said, "We're so excited Ryan's getting the Hensley-Robinson Award. My brother can't wait to host the party."

"He recently married, didn't he? My mother mentioned that."

"Yes, a few days ago."

Although Ryan had been fairly quiet up until this point, now he added, "Violet has another brother who got married the same day. When will Jessica and Clyde be back from their honeymoon?"

"Next week some time. The woman my brother Clyde married was a friend of mine. I can't wait until she gets back so we can really visit."

"After the experience she had, she and Clyde deserve a long honeymoon." Lily went on to explain to Lanie how Jessica had been stalked and how Clyde had apprehended the man.

As Rosita served brunch, the conversation flowed easily. Lanie filled them in on details of the gala her father would be attending and the security measures that would be taken.

They'd finished the fruit tart and were enjoying more coffee when Rosita appeared in the courtyard again and stood beside Ryan. "Chuck called from the barn. He said that horse you're going to gentle just rolled in."

Ryan looked torn as if he wanted to go down to the barn, yet knew he should stay because of Lanie.

Obviously sensing his predicament, she smiled. "Mr. Fortune, if you need to leave, that's fine. I have to be going myself. I have an appointment back in Austin this afternoon."

As she rose, so did Ryan. "Are you sure you have to leave so soon? My foreman can unload the horse."

"Really, I must be going," Lanie said. "It was nice to meet you, Violet."

After goodbyes all around, Ryan said, "I'll walk you out." Then he gave Lily a quick kiss and escorted the governor's daughter through the great room. After Rosita cleared the table except for the coffee, she took the tray of dishes to the kitchen.

Lily gave Violet a weak smile that told Violet brunch had been an effort. "That young woman doesn't seem to have a path to her life," Lily commented.

"Maybe some women don't need one."

"I found my path when I married Ryan." That troubled look came over Lily's face again. "But I wouldn't change one curve or twist in the path. Sometimes I wonder if Ryan would, though."

"I don't understand."

"I'm worried about him. He had a call from the police again this morning. They want him to come in for more questions. I wish they'd understand he didn't even *know* Christopher Jamison. Why can't they see he'd never hurt anyone?"

That was the question of a loyal wife, but Violet knew the authorities had their own agenda. The link between the Fortunes and Jamisons hadn't been made public, but there was one. She just hoped that the authorities would soon find the murderer of Christopher Jamison and that Ryan would be cleared.

"The two of you usually draw together when there's a crisis," Violet reminded Lily.

"Up until now. But Ryan's so unpredictable sometimes. For the past few months he leaves and doesn't tell me where he's going. I'm beginning to wonder—"

Her voice caught and Violet could see tears well up in Lily's eyes. One thing she was sure of—Ryan Fortune adored his wife and would never be unfaithful to her.

"Maybe he doesn't tell you because he doesn't know where he's going to go. Maybe he just needs time alone to decompress. Have you talked to him about it?"

"Yes, but he just gives me flimsy excuses."

"Maybe they seem flimsy because he's not hiding anything."

"I hope that's true," Lily said fervently.

Since Ryan was hiding his symptoms from his wife, that was why Lily suspected he wasn't being truthful. Maybe soon that would change. After the MRI, she hoped Ryan would tell Lily about his headaches and they could get their marriage back on a strong footing again. They might need to for whatever came next.

When Jason Jamison opened the door to his "mansion," he considered why he'd bought it when he moved to San Antonio. It was befitting the station in life he intended to rise to. The second reason, just as important, was that Melissa had liked it. She might have been a cocktail waitress, but she had damn good taste. Noticing the security alarm was off, he realized she must be at home. It was early for him to get home, not even six-thirty. He made a point of working late at Fortune TX, Ltd. so he looked like a go-getter, so he caught Ryan Fortune's attention, so he could put everything into the plan that was coming to fruition.

When he heard the upstairs shower running, he dropped his briefcase in the marble-floored foyer and hurried up the wide sweeping staircase. His footsteps were muffled by the plush carpeting, and he liked the idea of surprising Melissa. *He* didn't like surprises but he liked taking others off guard. He especially looked forward to surprising Ryan Fortune.

He was working on a plan to bring down Ryan and get the revenge his grandfather had always wanted. His grandpa Farley was the only one who had understood him and paid attention to him. During his visits to Farley Jamison's cabin, Jason had been a rapt listener when his grandfather related tales of Iowan politics. Farley's own children and wife had abandoned him. Although they were connected by blood, Kingston Fortune hadn't wanted anything to do with him, either. Someone had to carry on his grandfather's legacy. Farley had always believed it was because of the Fortunes that he was living his life in a beat-up shack, and he'd convinced Jason to believe it, too.

But Jason had to figure the best way to get what he wanted. With a new face, he was unrecognizable to relatives. Creating a different identity and going under the name of Jason Wilkes, he could accomplish anything.

As he walked down the hall, he took off his suit jacket and loosened his tie. One of his teachers in high school had called him a sociopath. If stabbing a friend and lying to get what he wanted made him that, he didn't mind the label. His conscience didn't bother him one whit that he'd killed Christopher. They'd always been like Cain and Abel, the angel and the devil. So much for angels, he thought, as he remembered dumping his brother's body into Lake Mondo.

After he stepped into the luxuriously furnished bedroom, Jason tossed his tie and suitcoat over a fuchsia chair, hurriedly unbuttoned his shirt and threw that to the pile, too. He couldn't wait to get his hands on Melissa. He couldn't wait to feel her hands on him. She knew how to do things—

Flipping off his Italian loafers, ridding himself of his socks, he unbuckled his belt as he went through the dressing room into the bathroom. There was a sunken tub, but his gaze went straight to the shower where he could see the shadow of Melissa's body behind the frosted glass door.

Before he could open it, she turned off the water and stepped out.

"Jason!" she yelped.

"That's me," he said with a smile that was supposed to convey his intentions.

It must have done just that because she shook her head, her bleached blond hair falling in wet tendrils across her shoulders. She hadn't dried off and she looked sleek and more than ready for what he had in mind.

However, she nipped his desire before he could act on it. "I can't. Not now. I'm already running late. I have a meeting at seven-thirty."

"What meeting?" he demanded to know.

"A group of us is getting together to plan a clothing drive for the teen shelter at Christmas."

"All this charity work you're doing is getting tedious, and I'm beginning to wonder why you're doing it."

Still dripping wet, Melissa came very close to Jason. "Aren't we pretending to be an up-and-coming married couple?"

"Yes, but—"

She put a slim finger on his chin and studied him with her brown eyes. "No buts. Just as you're setting up Ryan to take the fall for mistakes in his company, I'm planting a few seeds of my own."

"And they are?"

"You'll see." With the same finger that had played on his chin, she traced his right cheekbone. "How *is* your project coming?"

"It's moving along. Fortune TX, Ltd. is spending money on a phony oil deal and Ryan's fingerprints are going to be all over it."

"Do you really think they'll kick Ryan off the board of directors?"

"That's what I'm hoping."

Gazing into Melissa's eyes, Jason saw a flicker of something. What was it? Was she planning something on her own? How would that affect *him?*

Melissa never let him get too close or see too far inside. Now her hand settled on his chest then slipped lower, over his navel and inside the waistband of his trousers. "Maybe I do have ten minutes," she murmured with a wide-eyed, sultry look that aroused him to a painful level.

Taking the foreplay out of her hands, he scooped her into his arms. She was wet and wild and hot.

"Ten minutes," she warned him as he carried her into the bedroom.

He dropped her on the bed, let his trousers fall, pushed down his briefs and stretched out on top of her.

"It'll take what it's going to take, and your meeting be damned."

When he saw the look of triumph in her eyes, he knew this was what she'd wanted all along. As she opened her legs to him and kissed him like there was no tomorrow, he had to wonder who really had the power here.

He was going to get it back…one way or another.

It was almost 4:00 p.m. on Tuesday when Peter finally got the chance to call Violet Fortune. Still in his scrubs, he used the phone in the doctor's lounge. As her cell phone rang, he didn't have to use many memory cells to conjure up her face. He'd been thinking about her too damn much since she'd left last night, and he didn't like the invasion into his usually ordered thoughts.

There were several reasons why she should be off-limits for him. Number one—he no longer dated women whose career demands consumed their lives. He'd gone that route once

before, and once in a lifetime down that particular road was enough. Number two—not only
did Violet Fortune have a demanding career, but
the career was in New York. In a few weeks,
she'd return to New York City and pick up her
life where she'd left it. Long-distance relationships didn't work. His life, family and future
were here in Red Rock. Number three—Violet
Fortune rocked his world a little too much. He
liked to be in control. Last night, being around
her had thrown him off balance. It was an odd
feeling that hadn't happened to him before, not
even with his ex-fiancée Sandra.

"Hello," came a breathless voice after the
fourth ring.

"Violet? It's Peter Clark."

"Oh, Peter. Hi."

He heard the rustle of bags. "Did I catch you
at a bad time?"

"No, this is fine. I was just setting down the
groceries. I stopped at the store on the way back
from the Double Crown."

"You saw Ryan today?"

"Yes. I had brunch with him and Lily and
the governor's daughter. But we didn't have a
chance to talk. Lily's so worried about him. She
sees the stress he's under. She and I went riding

this afternoon and I'm afraid she's imagining all kinds of things."

"Hopefully, soon we can put both of their minds to rest. My colleague in Houston has made arrangements for Ryan's MRI on Saturday. We have to be there by ten. Since our appointment with him for the results is later in the day, I'm wondering if we should stay in Houston overnight. Ryan might be tired. Can you talk to him about it and see how he feels? I can clear my schedule to drive back Sunday morning. One of my partners can cover for me."

"With no questions asked?"

"With no questions asked."

A multitude of questions raced through his head concerning Violet. He wondered what her life had been like growing up with Lacey and Patrick Fortune and four brothers. As the only daughter, had she been a tomboy? Somehow he doubted that.

"I'll talk to Ryan," Violet assured him. "He mentioned that he and Lily will be attending a fund-raiser for San Juan Hospital at the Madison Hotel on Friday night. He told me the money would be used for high-tech equipment in the pediatrics wing that's a memorial to your mother."

"Ryan and Lily have always been supportive

of fund-raising attempts for the pediatrics wing. Lily was instrumental in helping me launch the first fund drive."

Despite the good cause, this was one event Peter didn't want to be reminded of, thanks to his sisters and that god-awful bachelor auction. In spite of himself, he couldn't help asking, "Will you be attending the fund-raiser with them?"

"I'm thinking about it. My brother Miles is one of the bachelors being auctioned off."

"I wonder who bribed him," Peter grumbled.

"Uh-oh," she said with a laugh. "Does that mean somebody bribed you?"

"No, with me it was blackmail. My sisters warned me that if I didn't volunteer, they'd list my name in the personal ads on the Internet."

When Violet began laughing again, he liked the sound of it. He didn't feel at all as if she were laughing at him, but rather laughing *with* him.

Finally, she said, "Thank you, Peter. That felt good. I haven't had much to smile about lately."

"Because you're worried about Ryan?"

"Yes." She paused then went on, "I came to Red Rock to get away from my practice for a little while."

"That burnout we discussed?"

There was more silence and he suddenly wondered if she'd confided in anyone about her real reasons for coming to Red Rock. Irrationally, he wanted her to confide in him.

"Yes."

When she didn't go on, he said, "Burnout happens."

"I guess it does, but this time when I lost a patient, not only her husband questioned my judgment. I did, too."

"You're a perfectionist," he said kindly, without criticism.

"Aren't you?" she shot back. "Don't we *have* to be?"

The first day they'd talked, he'd felt a bond with Violet because of Ryan. Now he realized they had another bond, too—their work. "We have to use our skill the best way we know how. We can be perfectionists but we're not God."

When she took a deep breath, he heard it. As doctors, they had power, but sometimes they didn't realize their power was finite.

"You're right, of course," she murmured. "And usually I take what happens in stride. For the past couple of months I haven't been able to do that. I took a cruise to get some perspective."

"Did it help?"

"It was a distraction but no, it didn't help."

"Maybe once we know what's going on with Ryan you'll find perspective again."

"Maybe." She sounded doubtful.

Peter's pager beeped. "I'm being paged," he said to Violet. "Hold on a minute."

Seeing the extension number, he knew he had to go. "I have to check on a patient, Violet."

"I know the sound of a pager when I hear it," she assured him with complete understanding. "I'll talk to Ryan and one of us will be in contact with you."

In spite of the conversation they'd just had, Peter hoped that person would be Ryan. Violet Fortune was simply too interesting, too intriguing and too beautiful for his peace of mind.

However, when he said goodbye, he wondered if *she* would be at the bachelor auction Friday night.

Whether she was or wasn't didn't matter. He was going to sleepwalk through it, get it over with and take whoever bought him to the Riverwalk the following weekend. That would be his contribution to charity.

Giving up fistfuls of money would be a hell of a lot easier.

As Peter headed to the third floor to answer his page, he couldn't sweep Violet from his thoughts. At least not until he stopped at the nurses' desk in Pediatric ICU, learned which patient needed him and went down the hall to Celeste Bowlan's room. The six-year-old was crying and nothing the nurses tried could console her. For whatever reason, Peter's presence always seemed to calm her. He strode toward her bed now, his heart going out to the little orphan with the straggly straight black hair, bangs and huge dark eyes.

"Hey there," he said softly. "Nurse Carmelita told me you're having a bad day."

When Celeste turned her tearstained face to his, he saw her desolation and sorrow. Over a year ago she'd been staying with a babysitter when her parents, who had gone out for the evening, had been involved in a three-car pileup. They'd both died on impact.

Celeste had been entered into the system and placed with a foster family. But her foster family hadn't cherished her as her parents had. Apparently her foster father had been a closet alcoholic who'd been driving drunk with Celeste in the car. They'd been in an accident, and Celeste's back had been fractured. Along with spinal injuries, a lung had collapsed, and she'd experienced belly trauma. Peter was going to operate to fuse her spine, but he had to wait until she was more stable.

The social worker on Celeste's case had told him she wouldn't be going back to that foster family, but another hadn't been found yet. Unable to walk and absolutely alone in the world, she was desolate with good reason. He tried to visit her as often as he could.

Pulling up a chair beside her bed, he brushed a few tears from her cheek. "Come on now. Let's see if you can stop crying so we can talk."

Sedated and on pain meds, Celeste was groggy. Slowly she complained, "You didn't come in all day."

He felt a stab of guilt, but he really hadn't had a spare moment.

"I know, but I had patients to see. They need help just as you do. I was going to come in tonight, though. I promised, remember? You said you'd pick out two books and I was going to read both of them to you."

"Will you still come tonight?"

He had to smile. If Celeste could get two visits out of this, she was going to do that.

"Sure, I'll come back later." He heard the med cart being pushed by a nurse rattle across the tile in the hall. "First I just have to grab something to eat and make some phone calls."

Her face fell and he saw tears well up again.

"On the other hand, I could buy a sandwich from the vending machine and eat it here," he said. "Then you can tell me what videos you watched today."

The room had a VCR, and Peter could see from the stack on the table that the nurses had picked out quite a few for Celeste. "I'll be back as soon as I find some food."

"Promise?" she asked.

He held up his hand like a Boy Scout. "I promise."

All at once his conversation with Violet came to mind, and he remembered what she'd told him about being burnt out. Maybe *she* would consider spending some time with Celeste. A woman with time on her hands might be just what the little girl needed. He'd broach that subject when they took Ryan for his tests or if she came to the fund-raiser Friday evening.

Insisting to himself again that he didn't care if she came or not, he went on a search for supper.

Chapter 3

The hotel ballroom was sumptuously elegant. Guests sat on champagne-colored brocade chairs at tables covered with pale rose tablecloths. Candles at each table as well as the overhead crystal chandeliers sent sparkles of light dancing off reflective surfaces.

Violet was seated with Lily and Ryan, her brother Miles and some friends of his. Often Violet's gaze went to Ryan. He was looking worn and tired tonight, and she was concerned because his headaches might be getting worse. She was glad Peter had been able to arrange the MRI for tomorrow morning. Ryan had told Lily he was taking a trip to Houston for business. After he'd given her the name of the hotel where they'd be staying, she'd accepted the explanation. But Violet could see the tension the lies were causing.

A chamber group had been playing softly throughout dinner and now they quieted at the bustling activity on the stage. A woman tapped on the microphone a few times, smiled at the audience and said, "I want to welcome everyone to the Estelle Clark Memorial Fund-Raiser."

The woman at the mike looked about Violet's age. There was something about her that seemed familiar. She was a tall, striking brunette who had a beautiful sense of fashion. Her emerald chiffon gown flowed around her body as if it had been designed especially for her.

Lily leaned close to Violet. "Stacey owns a boutique in the Galleria. I shop there a lot. Besides that, she's—"

Stacey was speaking again and Lily's words were drowned out. "As many of you know, it's an honor for me to be here, happy to raise money to buy equipment for my mother's memorial wing."

Suddenly it all clicked into place for Violet, why she thought the woman looked familiar. She was Estelle Clark's daughter and

Peter's sister. Although Violet had been pre-occupied with other thoughts, she'd gotten a quick glimpse of her and another woman as they'd left Peter's office. That must have been his other sister. At Peter's house she'd seen a picture of them in the pine cupboard, but they'd been much younger and Violet hadn't made the connection.

Stacey continued, "And now, so I won't bore you, I'll get to the highlight of this evening—our very eligible bachelors. Mr. Kinsdale, come on up on stage."

A tall, blond man in his thirties climbed the steps and came to stand near the microphone. When he smiled, Stacey motioned him to walk to the end of the short runway.

"Let them get a gander at you. Mr. Kinsdale's lucky benefactor will win a day of golf at his country club along with dinner overlooking the eighteenth hole. Let's start the bidding at one hundred dollars."

The bids came fast and furious. Women at two particular tables were doing much of the bidding.

"They're nurses," Lily explained with a smile. "I understand most of them have saved up all year for this donation."

The bidding ended at two thousand dollars.

"You should bid," Lily urged Violet as one gentleman after another walked to the edge of the runway.

"I'm not sure that's the best way to get a date," Violet joked. "I think I'd rather just write a check for the equipment—"

However, when she saw Peter Clark step up onto the stage, she stopped midsentence. He was a sight in a tuxedo. Although he looked totally debonair, he also looked uncomfortable.

Stacey Clark's voice took on a teasing liveliness as she gave her brother a quick appraisal. "Here we go, ladies. I have the fun of putting my brother on display tonight. I had to talk long and hard to get him to do this so don't disappoint me. I want this bid to go sky-high."

Lowering her voice, she said conspiratorially into the microphone, "He has a big ego. We wouldn't want it to get dented, would we? Come on, ladies. For a date at the Riverwalk with Dr. Peter Clark, let's start this bidding at two hundred dollars."

Peter's stride was confident though a bit stiff as he walked to the end of the runway, and Violet suspected that he hated being put on display. He must truly love his sister to do this for her. Violet had to admire his attempt at a winning smile, the thumbs-up sign he gave the audience that told them he was doing this in the spirit of fun.

The nurses started the bidding again but this time Violet couldn't keep quiet. Her hand shot up with the number she'd been assigned in case she wanted to bid, and she called out, "Five hundred."

Lily's elbow nudged hers. "Way to go."

Feeling her cheeks flush, she felt deflated when the bids kept rising above hers. Not knowing whether it was the competition urging her on or the desire to spend an evening at the Riverwalk with Peter, she helped push the price upward. Before she knew it, the bidding was up to twenty-five hundred dollars. One of the nurses, a petite blonde, wouldn't give up. Neither would Violet. They went back and forth in increments of fifty dollars until they hit three thousand.

"Well, well, ladies. It looks as if you'd like to give Peter a night to remember."

Violet didn't dare look at him, but she raised her bid and did it big. "Thirty-five hundred dollars," she called and the room went silent.

The nurse at the other table shook her head.

Stacey's face broke into a wide grin as she announced, "Number twenty-four has just won the honor of listening to my brother discuss medicine for an evening. Peter, make sure she has a little bit of fun, okay?"

Shaking his head with the tolerance of an older brother, he gave his sister a hug and descended the steps on the far side of the stage.

Violet wasn't sure exactly what to do.

"So go talk to him," Lily said with another nudge.

At least now she wouldn't have to pretend she and Peter were strangers. Maybe she could use that as an excuse for why she'd bid so enthusiastically.

Then she asked herself, *Why do you need an excuse?*

An inner voice whispered, *Because you don't want him to know you're attracted to him.*

Although her coral beaded gown had one very long slit from her thigh down to the hem, she didn't feel ladylike taking long strides. Warning herself not to hurry, to pretend a nonchalance she didn't feel, she found Peter at the rear of the stage talking to a woman she now recognized as Linda Clark.

When Peter's gaze fell on Violet, he took a good long look from her upswept hairdo to the pearls around her neck to the formfitting gown. The light that came into his eyes excited her, and she told herself to chill. Her work had always mattered more than relationships. Deep down, she knew she used work as an excuse to protect her heart, especially now when her life was in transition and she had to make some tough choices. Her stay in Red Rock was temporary and a short fling wasn't on her agenda. Despite all that, her pulse raced and excitement tingled up and down her spine as she moved closer to Peter.

"The woman who finally ended my misery," he said lightly. "Linda, meet Violet Fortune. Violet, this is my sister, Linda Clark."

Peter's sister was gracious and friendly as she shook Violet's hand and smiled. "You two should have a wonderful time on the River-walk." She waved to someone behind Violet. "If you'll excuse me, I have to be in ten places at once tonight. It was nice to meet you, Violet." She gave her brother a pat on the arm. "Don't be a stranger. Remember, Charlene and Dad's anniversary party next Sunday evening."

In the space of a second, Violet saw consternation slip over Peter's face, but then it was gone and she wondered if she'd seen it at all. Didn't he want to go to his dad's anniversary party?

They were standing in a room with about three hundred people, yet when she looked into

Peter's eyes it was as if they were stranded on a desert island all alone. That idea was fanciful and she had to put a stop to the thought now. "I bid on you to give a donation to a good cause and so you and I didn't have to pretend we were strangers around Ryan and Lily. I'll understand if you really don't want to go on a date."

"A date was part of the bargain," he said seriously. "I haven't been to the Riverwalk for a while, but if you really don't want to go—"

"I'd like to go," she hurried to say. "I just wanted to let you off the hook. It would almost be like a blind date."

"I'm not blind, Violet." His gaze as it passed over her made her stomach flip-flop, and she didn't know what to say to that.

"Do you plan to stick around here much longer?" he asked.

"I don't know. I have to pay for my bid."

"I'd like you to meet one of my patients. Would you come with me to San Juan Hospital?"

"Now?"

"Yep, right now."

She waved to her gown. "Dressed like this?"

"Believe me, no one's going to care."

He intrigued her with his request. "All right. I'll pay for you." She abruptly stopped. "I mean for our date…then I'll meet you in the lobby."

"I'll go with you. I want to give a donation of my own."

Then his hand was at her elbow and he was guiding her through the people and the tables.

Violet wasn't used to any man besides her father and brothers being protective of her, but as Peter's fingers scorched her skin, she glanced up at him, tall and strong and broad-shouldered. She felt a quickening inside she'd never felt before. What *was* wrong with her?

They had to wait in line at the table set up near the doors where other women were also paying for their bids.

"Did your sisters help organize this?" she asked.

"They certainly did. They've been very involved with the pediatrics wing ever since it was built."

"They did a wonderful job. Is your father here?"

"No," Peter said tersely. Then when he realized that had sounded sharp, he offered, "After my mother died, my father went on with his life."

"That's a good thing, right?" Violet prompted, hoping Peter would reveal more.

"That depends on how you look at it. He remarried less than a year after my mother died."

"How old were you?"

"I was thirteen, Stacey was eleven, and Linda was nine."

"I'm sorry, Peter. I can't imagine losing a parent at my age now, let alone when I was that young."

The line had dwindled away and now the woman at the table collecting checks looked up expectantly at Violet.

Peter took his checkbook from an inside jacket pocket and she knew the conversation was closed. Maybe that was best. She and the doctor were colleagues in Ryan's care and she should keep it at that.

A few minutes later they were walking through the lobby of the hotel when Peter commented, "I only caught a few glimpses of Ryan, but he looked tired tonight. Are his symptoms becoming any more pronounced?"

"Not that I've noticed, but he's used to hiding them from Lily."

"What did he tell her about staying in Houston overnight?"

"She thinks he's having dinner with business associates and then a late meeting."

The doorman held the door for them as they stepped into the night. Peter gestured to the parking area at the side of the hotel and removed a remote control from his trouser pocket. When a black SUV beeped, Violet knew which vehicle was his. She remembered seeing it in his garage the other night. To her surprise and pleasure, he opened the door for her. As she climbed in, the slit on her dress opened wide.

"So those things have a practical purpose," he noted in a wry tone.

The panel of the dress had slipped to the side, giving him a good look at her thigh and leg. She'd worn a dress like this before. She'd felt men's gazes on her before. But right now with Peter's eyes lighting with male appreciation, she felt self-conscious. Lifting the beaded material, she covered her leg on the pretense that she was protecting the fabric from the door. After Peter made sure she was safely tucked inside, he closed it.

Moments later her perfume mingled with the scent of his cologne in the car. Violet couldn't help but watch Peter's hand as he turned the key in the ignition then backed out of the parking space and drove through the parking lot. His hands were large, his fingers were long, and she could imagine his expertise in surgery. Unfortunately, she could imagine a lot more. How long had it been since a man had touched her... *really* touched her?

"Ever been to San Juan Hospital?" he asked.

"I was in the E.R. a few years ago when Miles had a run-in with barbed wire and needed stitches."

"Ouch."

Violet smiled. "That's not exactly what he said."

At Peter's chuckle, she asked, "Do you know my brothers?"

"I met Steven at one of Ryan and Lily's New Year's Eve parties. Your other brothers in passing."

"Were you at Steven and Amy's wedding?" Her brother had found the love of his life. When they had gotten married about a week ago, she hadn't seen Peter among the guests.

"I had just arrived when I got a call from the hospital. I had to leave before the wedding even got started. I heard your brother Clyde got married, too."

"Yep, he sure did. They'll be back from their honeymoon next week. Steven and Amy only took a few days because they want to get his new ranch in order for the party honoring Ryan."

"I heard he's receiving the Hensley-Robinson Award. He deserves it."

Peter turned into the hospital's parking lot.

Instead of heading for the parking garage, he veered toward the side of the building where signs marked the slots for physicians.

A few minutes later a security guard at the sliding glass doors nodded at Peter and gave Violet an interested glance. Her long gown obviously wasn't a usual sight at the hospital. As Peter guided Violet through the deserted lobby, he nodded to an older woman sitting at the information desk.

"Good evening, Myra."

"Good evening yourself, Dr. Clark. Spiffy getup. I'm glad to see you've been somewhere other than this hospital. He works too many hours," she confided to Violet as if she'd known her all her life.

"I hear doctors have that problem," Violet responded with a straight face.

"See you later, Myra," Peter said with a wave as he cupped Violet's elbow and guided her toward the elevators.

His touch sent electricity up her arm, and she wondered what he looked like under that tuxedo. When her cheeks grew hot, she banished the thought. She didn't know what had gotten into her since she'd met Peter Clark, but she didn't like it. Since she was a teenager, her head had ruled her life, not hormones, not her heart, not any other part of her. That wasn't going to change now.

When the elevator doors swished open, they stepped inside. Peter pressed the button for the third floor. Seconds later, they were there, exiting the elevator, turning left toward the sign that directed them to the pediatrics wing.

As they walked down the white-and-tan tiled floor, Violet had to ask herself what she was doing here with Peter. What had made her say yes to his invitation without even knowing whom they were going to see?

Instead of heading down the hall toward the general pediatrics unit, he took another turn and was suddenly in Peds ICU. Bright fluorescent lights glowed above the nurses' station, though the hall lights were a bit dimmer. The ICU rooms, directly across from the nurses' desk, were fronted with glass.

Peter's hand grazed the small of Violet's back. "I want to check a chart. I'll be just a minute."

While she was still trying to compose herself from the brush of his hand, he stepped behind the counter, greeted the nurse on duty, took a chart from the rack and examined it.

A few minutes later he was by her side again. "We're going to see Celeste Bowlan. She's six and doesn't have anybody to care about her except a social worker...and me. She was in an accident with her foster father who was driving drunk. Needless to say, she won't be going back to that couple. When the ambulance brought her in, she had a collapsed lung and a fractured back as well as abdominal bruising. I couldn't do surgery immediately. I've got it planned for Monday morning. She's stable now, but I have her sedated.

"When she looks at me with her big brown eyes, she about breaks my heart. She needs somebody to care about her, maybe visit her. Until after her surgery, it's only fifteen minutes on the hour, but it'll be something. I thought maybe since you have time on your hands—"

Violet felt herself going cold all over. She stood stock-still when Peter moved to one of the cubicles.

He glanced over his shoulder. "What's the matter?"

"I'm... I'm not sure you should have brought me here."

"Why not?"

"Because maybe I don't want to get involved."

Quizzically he studied her. "Because of the patient you lost," he guessed perceptively.

"That's part of it. Since then I've…pulled back."

"You mean you've detached yourself from your patients," he guessed.

"I haven't seen that many patients since it happened."

"Celeste is six years old and she's all alone," he said simply. "Reading a story to her now and then, just talking to her could do her a world of good."

"The mind-body connection?" Violet asked, knowing some doctors believed in it and some didn't.

"Absolutely."

Peter was obviously a doctor who did.

He was studying her with far too much intensity. She felt turned inside out and didn't like it, but she knowingly couldn't walk away and somehow he'd guessed that.

"Where is she?" Violet murmured.

He gestured toward cubicle number two. When he pushed the button on the wall, the glass door slid silently open. He crossed the threshold first and Violet hesitated only for a moment, then she stepped inside, too. The door closed behind them.

Equipment beeped and buzzed—monitors, the dispenser for the IV, the blood pressure cuff.

"Dr. Clark?" a small voice asked.

"You're supposed to be asleep," he scolded gently as he went to the head of the bed and switched on a small night-light.

"Read me a story?" Celeste asked in a sweet, childlike voice that wrapped itself around Violet's heart.

"I think it's too late for a story, but I brought someone to meet you."

Stepping up beside him, Violet looked down at Peter's small patient. Her eyes were dark brown and huge under her bangs. Her shoulder-length hair was absolutely straight. Violet longed to brush it for her, to soothe her, to somehow make it all better. But that was the problem. Doctors couldn't always make it all better. She'd found that out the hard way too many times.

Leaning close, Violet laid her hand on the little girl's, the one that didn't have an IV line. "I'm Violet," she said softly. "Dr. Clark tells me your name is Celeste. That's a beautiful name."

"My mommy and daddy picked it out," the little girl said proudly. Tears came to her eyes. "Mrs. Gunthry told me they're in heaven. I want to go to heaven, too."

A lump formed in Violet's throat and her heart felt as if it were cracking.

From behind her, Violet heard, "Mrs. Gunthry is Celeste's social worker."

Leaning a bit closer, gently brushing Celeste's bangs aside, Violet said, "I'll bet your mommy and daddy are very proud of you."

Celeste's eyes grew a little more focused. "Why?"

"Because you're being a very brave little girl. I'm sure they're watching over you and hoping you'll get better."

"How?"

From Violet's dealings with children in her practice, she knew they had endless questions and she didn't always have the answers. Violet lightly touched the little girl's chest. "They're always going to live in your heart and help you be strong and good and successful."

"Will they help me walk again?"

This time Violet looked at Peter since she didn't know Celeste's prognosis.

"You're going to walk again, Celeste," he said with determined certainty. "And they're going to be watching you do it. It might take a little while, but you're going to have lots of help."

"You?" she asked, her eyes drooping again.

"Me and other nurses and doctors and therapists." Peter checked his watch. "Violet and I are going to go now and let you sleep."

"Don't go," she whispered.

"I'll be back," Peter promised. "I have to take Violet back to her car, but then I'll come in and sit with you for a while. Okay?"

"'Kay," Celeste murmured as her eyelids closed.

Violet couldn't help but touch the little girl's cheek. There was a longing in her heart to do something for Celeste, and she knew she'd be back to visit.

Outside the cubicle, Peter explained, "The medication makes her sleepy. That's best under the circumstances."

"She is a heartbreaker," Violet admitted, her voice catching. As she walked down the hall, she asked, "Are you really coming back?"

"I always do what I say I'm going to do."

The assurance in Peter's voice made her believe him. She didn't know when she'd last met a man like him. He was kind...as well as downright sexy.

"I'd like to come back and visit her."

A smile played on his lips. "I was counting on it."

"You think I have too much free time on my hands?"

"Don't you?"

"I don't know. It's been nice not to have to adhere to a rigid schedule."

Stopping when they reached the elevator, he pressed the button. "You're young to have the reputation you've gotten. You've been working plenty hard."

The interior of the elevator seemed intimately confining when they stepped inside. As Peter glanced at her, their gazes locked and the current between them could have lit up the whole hospital for at least a week. She didn't know why she was having this reaction to him and that frightened her as much as excited her. Fortunately, their ride was brief. The lobby was empty.

As they approached the double glass doors, Peter remarked, "The party at the hotel should still be in full swing."

"I hope Ryan makes some excuse to go home and get a good night's sleep."

Peter nodded. "Putting up a good front takes a lot of energy. He might decide to stay until everybody leaves just to prove to Lily nothing's wrong with him."

"We'll know tomorrow."

After they came out of the hospital, Violet saw a bench to the side of the portico and asked, "Can we sit here a few minutes? I want you to tell me Celeste's prognosis."

They could have had this discussion in Peter's SUV, but something about that was unsettling. Here in the open air, Violet was less distracted by his cologne...by his sheer male presence.

If he thought her request odd, he didn't show it.

When she sat on the black, wrought-iron bench, a gust of wind reminded her that fall would be slipping into winter soon. She shivered.

Peter must have noticed because he shrugged out of his tuxedo jacket. Before she could assimilate the almost intimate gesture, he slipped his coat around her and she caught the lapels. Now she could feel the tangible evidence of his body heat. Now his scent almost made her giddy.

Finally seated beside her, his knee grazing hers, he explained, "Her prognosis is up in the air, not because of her injury as much as because of her circumstances. I'm afraid she won't try to get better. She needs support and affection and people who really care about her."

"Is the social worker trying to find her another family?"

"*Trying* is the operative word. It's hard enough to place older children, let alone children who require the care Celeste will need. Her foster father not only drove drunk, but through an investigation Mrs. Gunthry discovered the couple left her alone a lot, too. Celeste has a great-aunt, but she's in her sixties, arthritic and apparently wants nothing to do with caring for a child. Especially since Celeste didn't inherit anything but a few pieces of secondhand furniture."

A great-aunt who had only financial concerns in mind would never be a good parent. Caring about Celeste already, Violet insisted, "Give me Celeste's best-case scenario."

The wind blew Violet's hair across her cheek and she brushed it away. When Peter's gaze followed the course of her hand, his eyes seemed to turn a darker, more mysterious green. How she wished she knew what he was thinking.

"In the best-case scenario, I'll fuse her spine. It's fractured at the L4-5 level. The cord is bruised, not severed. She'll spend ten days to two weeks in the hospital, then be transferred to a rehab facility. There she can get the therapy she needs to walk again. That could take anywhere from two to five months—some of that in outpatient therapy. You know nothing about this is absolute. That's why her state of mind is so important."

His shoulder was touching Violet's now. As she looked up at him, she murmured, "I'll spend some time with her, for as long as I'm here."

"Your attention and support will help."

"Actually, I think she'll be helping me as much as I'll be helping her. Medicine has become too rote for me—diagnosing conditions I can slow but not cure, making judgments, suggesting decisions that can have dire consequences as well as successful ones."

"You were trained to make judgments and suggest decisions."

"Yes, I was, wasn't I? But apparently I wasn't trained well enough to remove myself from my patients. I've got to learn how to do that."

"No, you don't."

Her gaze collided with his and she saw such certainty there.

"I'm not removed from Celeste. You saw that. Should I be?" He shook his head. "I don't think so. If I were removed, I wouldn't be as invested in the outcome."

"I don't know, Peter," she said with a sigh.

"Maybe you'll figure it out while you're in Red Rock."

"Maybe, or maybe I'll have to return to my practice and figure it out there."

When Peter studied her again, she felt warm

in spite of the night chill. She felt so excited, her breath caught. Like a teenager on her first date, Violet was uncertain where the evening would lead. All of it could lead to trouble, she knew. After all, she didn't indulge in recreational affairs. She never let hormones overrule her head. She didn't look for relationships because she'd found out at a young age what loving the wrong man could do to her life, to her heart, to her future.

Remembering the girl she'd once been didn't happen often. She didn't want the picture to play in her mind now, either. With a quick shrug, she escaped the warmth of Peter's jacket, gathered it and offered it to him.

"Thanks for letting me use this. I think I'd better get back."

His focus narrowed slightly but he didn't try to convince her to stay. Standing, he accepted the jacket and tossed it over his arm. Without another word, they walked to his car.

After he drove to the hotel in silence, he found his parking spot still empty.

Exiting his SUV, Violet said, "I'm not going inside. I'm going to drive back to the Flying Aces." She didn't feel like answering questions about where she'd been, why she'd left with

Peter, why she'd outbid every other woman in the room for him.

"I'll walk you to your car." It wasn't an offer or a request. It was a matter-of-fact statement that told her he wouldn't change his mind.

"I'm not afraid of the dark," she said in a teasing tone.

"Maybe you should be."

Since she lived in New York City, her attitude wasn't cavalier. She'd taken a self-defense course. Yet as she pointed out where she'd parked, she wasn't concerned about her safety as much as she was concerned about her attraction to Peter Clark.

Opening her purse, she took out her keys. After she pressed the remote control button, the car beeped. She stood at the driver's door not knowing exactly what to say to Peter. It had been an unusual evening.

She settled on, "I guess I'll see you tomorrow morning. I worry about Ryan driving if this is more than tension headaches. I told him I'd meet him outside the Double Crown and follow him to your place."

"Did Ryan tell you I'd like to leave by 6:30 a.m.?"

"Yes, he did."

"Will your brother question where you're going?"

"With me living at the pool house, we hardly notice each other's comings and goings. Miles doesn't watch over me as closely as Clyde does. He won't miss me."

The parking lot lights cast a combination of glow and shadows. Peter's gaze held hers. She couldn't seem to look away and neither could he. The awareness between them had her senses raised to a fever pitch.

When Peter bent toward her, she was afraid to breathe. She was afraid she'd break the spell. She was afraid his pager might interrupt or else he'd change his mind. In spite of warning bells clanging in her head, she wanted to feel his lips on hers. She wanted to taste him. She wanted to find out if the excitement between them was real.

At the moment his lips touched hers, she knew it was. One of his strong arms went around her and she lifted her lips into the kiss, telling him she wasn't going to pull away. The sexual tension that had been humming between them since they'd met had needed an outlet, but the kiss was much more than that.

Heat flashed through Violet, making even her fingertips tingle. Coherent thoughts vanished as her body simply responded to Peter's. His tongue was making her crazy with need. When her arms went around his neck, she pressed into him, and his taut body told her he was as aroused as she was. This kiss was so different from the inexpert kisses of her teenage years, so different from awkward first-date kisses, so different from the maybe-I'll-try-this-again kisses that had left her cold. She was going up in flames with Peter and she wondered where they could possibly go from here.

She never got the chance to find out. Suddenly the kiss ended as he dropped his arms and stepped away. When she glanced up at him, she was still trembling all over, but he looked as composed as he had all night.

He said, "That was probably not one of the more intelligent things I've ever done."

Her pride kept her from asking why, from showing him the effect he'd had on her. Her pride was something she could hold on to, wrap around herself and rely on.

"It was just a kiss," she said lightly as if it hadn't mattered at all.

When he cocked his head, she felt as if he were trying to see right through her, yet she knew he couldn't. She'd been building walls around herself all her life—since she'd been fifteen, pregnant and more alone than she'd ever felt in her entire existence. There was no way Peter could see into her heart, mind or head.

Opening the car door, she quickly slid inside and closed it. She did not roll her window down to say a final goodbye. Rather she started the engine, shifted the car into gear and backed up. She didn't even glance in her rearview mirror as she drove away.

Tomorrow morning, when she saw Peter again, she'd be prepared. They'd consult professionally about Ryan, then go their separate ways. End of story.

But her lips still felt as if they were on fire from his kiss, and her insides still quivered. When she felt tears come to her eyes, she took a deep breath and banished them. She was Violet Fortune, strong and independent. She didn't need a man.

She repeated that phrase like a mantra the whole way back to the Flying Aces.

Chapter 4

The auction was over and Jason Jamison gazed across the half-crowded room, glad he hadn't been up for bid. He'd briefly thought about being a high-priced bachelor, but then he remembered he was supposed to be married. He'd brought "his wife" to the shindig and they'd mingled with the right crowd. Except now she was mingling a little too much.

Melissa was fawning all over Ryan Fortune and nothing about it looked like pretend. She was supposed to be a partner in bringing the old guy down, but this didn't look like partnering to Jason. Her hand was intimately slipped around Ryan's arm and she was staring up into his face, wide-eyed, all coy seductress. Ryan's wife, Lily, looked on, seeming none too happy. She knew what Melissa was up to. Women had a sixth sense where that was concerned and Lily was no dummy.

Jealousy raged inside him as Melissa laughed and moved a little closer to Ryan. Her body language told Jason exactly what she was doing and he didn't like it. He didn't like it at all. He wanted to wring her beautiful neck.

Lily moved closer to Ryan's other side as if protecting her property.

Tired of the whole scenario, Jason spun on his heel before he did something he'd regret, and left the ballroom. He strode right out of the hotel. He didn't walk far, just enough to bring his boiling temperature down to a simmer. Staring out into the parking lot, he searched for his cigarettes, pulled out a pack with a lighter and ignited one of them. Then he inhaled deeply, trying to turn his anger and jealousy into something manageable, something more productive.

The gleam in Lily's eye as she'd watched Melissa had been as sharp as a dagger. Instead of reacting to his own jealousy, he should concentrate on Lily's and figure out how to use it to bring the Fortune family down.

Karen Rose Smith   85

* * *

Saturday morning Violet waited in her car
for Ryan a short distance from the access road
that led to the Double Crown. When his large
blue-and-silver crew cab truck pulled into view,
she followed him to Peter's. As prearranged,
she parked curbside in front of Peter's house
in her nondescript rental car.

Obviously watching for them, Peter opened
the garage, and Ryan pulled his truck inside.
She joined them there.

Five minutes later, they were riding in Peter's SUV toward Houston, Ryan in the pas-
senger seat. Worried about Ryan, she tried to
make polite conversation for a while. Finally it
dwindled away into silence, and Peter switched
on the satellite radio. No commercials, no talk,
just smooth jazz. There had been awkwardness
between her and Peter since their kiss last night
that not even anxiety over Ryan could diminish.

When they arrived at the Houston hospital,
Peter knew exactly where to go. They didn't
stop in registration but rather went to a doctor's
office on the second floor. The brass plate on
the door read Dr. Frank Grimaldi.

Once inside, a pretty blond receptionist
looked up at them. After Peter gave his name,

she didn't ask any more questions, just took a sheaf of papers from inside a file folder.

"Dr. Grimaldi will be with you shortly. Please have a seat."

The waiting room was decorated with comfortable cushioned furniture, a coffee table with the latest magazines, and low lighting. She and Peter sat, exchanged a glance much too full of everything that had happened the night before, and watched Ryan pace. Thankfully, a few minutes later, Dr. Grimaldi appeared.

After an enthusiastic handshake with Peter, a less energetic one for Violet, he turned to Ryan, shook his hand and assured him, "We intend to keep your identity a secret. You don't have to worry. Medicine is becoming more about ID numbers than names, anyway. Since you're paying cash, confidentiality will be absolutely assured."

"What happens first?" Ryan asked.

"I have you scheduled for an MRI in half an hour. I'd like you to come inside to one of the examination rooms and change into a hospital gown. I'll do a preliminary exam, then my receptionist will wheel you down to radiology."

Doffing his Stetson, Ryan ran his hand through his hair. "Let's get this over with. I want to know the verdict."

"You won't have the verdict until later this afternoon, right, Frank?" Peter asked.

"That's right. The MRI will take about an hour, maybe longer if we use dye, and I suggest you all get some lunch afterward and try to relax. I'll meet you back here at four."

"Are you going to wait here for me?" Ryan asked Violet.

"Yes. I'll try to catch up on the latest fads, gossip and miracle cures in the magazines."

"Good," Ryan said with a smile. "I might need one of those miracle cures."

Giving Ryan a hug, Violet didn't know what to say. She was hoping for the best and didn't even want to think about the worst. Ryan had always been a strong, vibrant presence in her life. She absolutely couldn't imagine anything happening to him and didn't want to.

"Go with Dr. Grimaldi," she whispered, her voice catching.

He patted her on the back as he would a child and then he followed the doctor down the hall to an examination room.

For the next twenty minutes, Violet felt as if she were going to jump out of her skin. Yes, her concern for Ryan was making her tense, but sitting in this small room with Peter wasn't helping, either. With the receptionist stationed at the desk, they weren't about to have a private conversation, assuming Peter *wanted* to have a private conversation. He seemed genuinely engrossed in a news magazine.

Was he always cool, calm, and collected? Didn't anything ruffle him? If she was up for a challenge, that would have been it—trying to ruffle Peter Clark. However, right now she just wanted to make time pass quickly. It wasn't.

Finally, Dr. Grimaldi himself wheeled Ryan into the reception area. Ryan was a tall man, husky, with plenty of muscles. But this morning, in that wheelchair with a cover over his lap, he looked…older, resigned, downright weary.

Violet went to him and crouched down by his side. When she gazed into his eyes, she couldn't say anything. Instead, she kissed his weathered cheek. For some reason the gesture of affection just seemed necessary.

The receptionist took hold of Ryan's chair and pushed it out the door.

Dr. Grimaldi said to Peter, "I'll see you later." He glanced at his watch. "I'm already late for a meeting. You're welcome to wait here if you'd like." Then he was gone, too.

It only took Violet a few moments to realize she couldn't sit here and read more magazines.

"I'm going to go stir-crazy if I stay here. Do you want to go for a walk?"

"That's probably a good idea. But I think we should talk first."

"About last night?" As soon as the question was out, she wished she hadn't asked because now he'd know it had been on her mind.

"About what happened in the parking lot." His voice went lower. "I should never have kissed you."

"I was there, too," she reminded him, waiting to hear his reasons why it was a bad idea. She had hers, but she wanted to know his.

He looked chagrined for a few moments but then with determination went on, "You're a beautiful woman, Violet, but you've got a high-powered career. Not only that, your career is in New York. I've been down that road before. It's not one I want to travel again. My guess is, you don't even know how long you'll be in Texas."

"I've cleared my schedule for a month."

"We can do a lot of damage in a month. We could disrupt our lives and tear up our emotions and at the end of it be sorry we ever met."

His conclusions about what would probably happen irked her. She couldn't help but say, "I'm glad you have a crystal ball. Do you know where *I* can buy one?"

His tone was wry. "No crystal ball. Just logic and a healthy dose of past experience."

"So you have a prejudice against career women?"

"I respect career women, and some careers don't consume twenty-four hours a day. But you and I both know our careers do. I guess what I'm saying, Violet, is that I'm looking for more than a good time rocking the bed."

If he was being brutally blunt to shock her, he didn't. "I dream about having it all someday," she admitted. "The truth is, no man has ever made me reconsider my goals or the time I spend with my patients. That might never change."

On the other hand, hadn't she come to Texas because the path she'd chosen didn't seem to fit anymore? Her pride kept her from expressing any of that to Peter. He already had his mind made up.

Finally that Fortune pride of hers made her say as she had last night, "It was just a kiss, Peter."

His gaze roamed hers for a long, silent moment, then he agreed, "It *was* just a kiss."

Before Violet could respond, the office door opened and a woman wearing a smock and carrying a large manila envelope came inside and went to the receptionist's office.

"Let's go for that walk," Peter urged, and Violet knew any personal conversation between them was now over. They would make small talk, converse about Texas and New York and Ryan. They'd ignore the electricity sparking between them because that was the safest route to take.

Violet wasn't sure the safe route felt like the right one any longer.

By the time Ryan's MRI was finished, tension between Peter and Violet was off the charts. Peter drove them to a small, quiet restaurant near their motel, not exactly knowing what to say or how to act with the pretty doctor. That kiss last night had practically untied his wingtips, not to mention revved him up enough that primitive caveman tendencies had almost taken over. He'd handled the kiss, the aftermath and Violet poorly. The simple truth was—he wasn't used to a woman giving him insomnia. He wasn't used to a woman making his world tilt. He wasn't used to a woman making him feel as if his control had slipped. On top of that, his gut told him what that MRI was going to say.

He parked in a space around the corner from the restaurant door. None of them spoke until they were seated at a table inside and a waitress had brought them menus.

Ryan glanced at his, closed it and laid it down on the place mat. "I'm not hungry."

"No matter what the results are of that MRI," Violet insisted, "you have to take care of yourself."

Peter noticed the deepening lines around Ryan's eyes and over his brows. "Do you still have a headache?"

"It was made ten times worse by the banging in that machine. Or by the dye they injected into me," Ryan grumbled.

"After we finish here, we can check in at the motel. I made arrangements for an early check-in so you can rest until our appointment with Dr. Grimaldi."

"What I need is some fine bourbon."

After lunch, Peter, Violet and Ryan went to their separate rooms. At three-thirty, they met in the lobby to return to the hospital. When they reached Dr. Grimaldi's office, the receptionist told them he'd be with them in a few minutes.

Ten minutes later, when Dr. Grimaldi came into the waiting area, his gaze fell on Ryan.

"Do you want this to be private, or do you want Dr. Clark and Dr. Fortune to be present also?"

Ryan stood. "I want them there."

Grimaldi motioned to them to follow him.

After Peter and Violet flanked Ryan in the chairs sitting before Grimaldi's desk, the neurosurgeon steepled his fingers on the blotter. Then his eyes met Ryan's.

Ryan said, "Keep this simple, Doc. I want to be able to understand it."

Dr. Grimaldi's attention went to Peter and then to Violet. "Ryan has a glioblastoma multiforme. The tumor is located deep in the brain and across the midline." His focus went back to Ryan. "In simple terms you have an inoperable brain tumor. The symptoms you're having now—headaches, some numbness in the left arm, coordination problems—will increase in severity, eventually including speech impairment, confusion and finally a coma. The statistics say you'll have three to six months."

"Inoperable?" Ryan repeated as if that were the only word he'd heard.

Although the diagnosis wasn't unexpected, Peter felt like he'd received a blow to the gut. Clasping Ryan's arm, he insisted, "It might be inoperable, but that doesn't preclude experimental treatment."

"Treatment like strange drugs and chemotherapy?" Ryan looked aghast.

"Possibly. Maybe radiation. There are many programs. I'm sure I can find something."

But before Peter was able to finish talking, Ryan was shaking his head. "No. None of that stuff. I don't want to be sicker, not before I have to be."

Peter knew the diagnosis was a shock and Ryan had to come to terms with everything that it implied. He could see Violet was in shock, too. She blinked rapidly, and he guessed she was holding back tears.

Dr. Grimaldi offered, "Peter's right about experimental treatment. If you want to search it out, I'm sure you can find it. I'll cooperate with anyone who needs records or results of the MRI. Just call me and let me know. You're going to need a physician close by in Red Rock—"

"No." Ryan's tone was adamant. "I'm not running to a doctor when nothing can be done, and certainly not before I tell anybody about this. I don't know when I'm going to do that."

"You should tell Lily," Peter advised somberly.

"Not yet. Not now. I have to think about all of it." Then Ryan stood and went to the door. "Send the bill for all this to Peter's office. I'll see that he gets the money." Then he was leaving and Violet was hurrying after him.

When Peter turned to Grimaldi, he saw sadness there. "We save patients lives, too," Peter reminded him as if he knew the doctor needed to hear it.

"That's no consolation to Ryan Fortune."

"No, it's not, but it might be some to you. The only way we can do this day after day is to remember the hope. I intend to give Ryan some hope. I'll find an experimental program and get him into it."

"Good luck," Grimaldi said. "You're going to need it because he's a stubborn man. It only takes five minutes with him to know he's going to do what he's going to do, no matter what anyone says."

"That's true. But after he thinks about this for a few days, I'm betting he'll choose hope over certain death."

Peter and Frank shook hands and slapped each other on the back.

"Let me know what he decides. Call me any time."

After a nod, Peter left the office. As he walked toward the reception area, he knew he was going to have to gather information quickly and present it to Ryan in a way he couldn't refuse. An experimental program might not save his life, but it could prolong it. Peter wanted Ryan to have countless days left, not just three to six months. But Ryan had to want that, too.

Peter made a stop on the return trip to the motel for Chinese takeout. He sensed Violet wanted to spend some time alone with Ryan. While they sat in the car, he went into the restaurant for the food.

In Ryan's room a half hour later, Peter wished he could give Ryan a good bottle of bourbon. But with a brain tumor, alcohol could trigger a seizure. At the table by the window, Violet worked at opening the take-out containers. The aromas of beef and broccoli, chicken lo mein, and Moo Goo Gai Pan filled the room. None of them was hungry, but he and Violet picked at their food in hopes that Ryan would eat, too. To their surprise, he did, but he also stared out the window and didn't have much to say. Peter knew the diagnosis was still unreal to him and it would take a while to absorb.

Out of the blue, Ryan said almost angrily, "Don't think I'm going to lie down and wait for this to happen. I have lots to do. Until I say so, no one breathes a word about this. Understood?"

"Understood," Peter and Violet both said in unison, though neither of them agreed.

"I want to get out of here early tomorrow," Ryan decided. "Can we leave by eight?"

"Eight's good," Peter agreed. "I need to get back as soon as I can to make rounds at the hospital."

When Violet took the last of the take-out containers into the bathroom and threw them in the trash can there, Peter knew she was too quiet. He was concerned about her reaction to the diagnosis. He knew she cared for Ryan deeply and wasn't just looking at his situation from a doctor's perspective.

After she picked up her purse, she gave Ryan a long, tight hug.

Taking a card from his pocket, Peter placed it by the phone. "No matter what time it is, you can reach me. I'll have my cell phone with me if I'm not in my room."

Ryan nodded at that, gratitude on his face. After he released Violet, she quickly walked to the door, opened it and stepped out into the hall.

When Peter followed her, he asked, "Stairs or the elevator?"

"Stairs," she decided in a quick tone and headed that way.

Feeling the need for physical exertion, too,

he was well aware a flight of stairs wouldn't be nearly enough.

At the door to Violet's room, Peter noticed her rigid posture as she used her key card to open the door. His instincts urged him to follow her inside.

The decor of Violet's room was almost identical to his. The geometrically designed bedspread and drapes in navy, green and rust, the requisite dark wood dresser, entertainment center and chest, desk and table for two. Violet crossed to the table by the window and set her purse there. She didn't turn around but rather stared out at the evening setting in, the traffic going by, the live oaks lining the perimeter of the motel property.

Peter closed the door. When he came to stand behind her, he saw the quiver of her shoulders and heard the catch of her breath as she bowed her head.

"Violet," he said softly, knowing Ryan's diagnosis was eating her up inside. She had to let it out. When she shook her head and swiped at her cheek, Peter couldn't help putting his arm around her.

"I have to be strong for him," she murmured. "I have to be strong for my family. I can't—" Her voice broke on the word and he held her tighter until she turned into his chest and let the tears fall.

Guiding her to the bed, he sat beside her, his arm around her.

When her tears wouldn't slow, she held her face in her hands, covering it so he wouldn't see. "I love him, Peter. He's like a second dad. I just can't believe this."

"I haven't known him as long as you have, so I can't say I understand what you're feeling. But I do know what it's like to lose someone important to you."

"That's the problem, Peter, the losing. Don't you get tired of it?"

"I don't always lose. Sometimes I win."

Already she was shaking her head. "Not often enough, at least not lately. Those two women I diagnosed with MS… One is a young mother of two. The other is earning her doctorate in African studies. She wants to work for the UN and help the children. Sure, there are better treatments now for conditions I diagnose, but at the end of the day, I can't cure them."

She paused and finally added, "Then there was Anne."

Tears continued to slip down Violet's cheeks and her voice was thick with emotion, remembrance and regret. "She was pregnant and I diagnosed an aneurysm. I suggested she see a neurosurgeon with whom we consulted. We advised her to have surgery because she was in her second trimester. She and her husband put their trust in us. On the operating table, the aneurysm burst and she bled out. We lost her *and* her baby."

It didn't take long to see what kind of doctor Violet was. She cared, maybe too damn much, and she took responsibility over areas she couldn't control. She hadn't been in the operating room working on this Anne, the neurosurgeon had, yet she was accepting blame as if she had performed the surgery.

"When she died, her husband told me it was my fault because Anne trusted me."

"Your patients have to trust you or you won't be effective."

"I know that, but I just wish—"

"You wish you could cure them all."

When their gazes met and held, Violet turned her face up to his. He wanted to kiss her so badly that all his earlier reasoning seemed inconsequential. Sure they could undress, have sex and forget about all the bad stuff for a short while. But then what?

Brushing his hand over her cheek, he kissed her forehead.

"I'm just so tired, Peter," she murmured. "So tired of not having the answers, of keeping a lid on my emotions, of not being able to help enough."

Most days, Peter's passion for his work won out above all else. But there were others when he felt like Violet did now—bone weary, tired to his soul, unsure whether the sun would rise tomorrow. For some totally illogical reason, he felt as if he'd known Violet for much longer than a week. A bond from Ryan and their work had formed on top of a chemistry that bubbled between them. That was why he continued to hold her.

That was why a few minutes later, he shifted on the bed, stretched out and opened his arms to her. "Come on. I'll hold you for a while. Just hold you. Maybe if you share the burden, it won't seem so huge."

At first she looked as if she was going to refuse, and he was prepared for that. But then she stared at the crook of his arm, let out a deep breath and curled up beside him. She was rigid at first, but as he stroked her hair, she relaxed.

"This isn't like me, Peter," she mumbled. "I don't usually need anyone."

As he continued stroking her hair and her breaths became slower and deeper, he couldn't help but wonder why Violet wouldn't let herself need anyone.

It was better not to ask.

If he asked, he'd become more involved than he already was.

Chapter 5

Violet had never felt so safe…so warm…so protected.

Protected? Why would she need to be protected?

Then she remembered yesterday, the neuro-surgeon's diagnosis, Ryan's pale face, her melt-down last night and… Peter.

He was holding her. She didn't know if they'd ever moved out of their spoon position. His arm was tucked around her waist, his jaw was nestled onto the top of her head, his muscled lean body was loosely molded to hers. Before she'd fallen asleep, she'd felt him aroused against her, yet he'd made no move to act on that arousal.

And she knew why. He was a disciplined man. He was also practical and forward-looking. If they became involved, their lives would take on complications that neither of them needed.

Her aim now was to slip out of the bed without disturbing him. Yet as soon as she even thought about scooting away from him, his arm shifted slightly and his voice was low above her head.

"Are you awake?"

Self-preservation had made her dwell on his comfort rather than his male scent, his large hand close to her hip, his powerful thighs against her backside. Now she couldn't preserve even the illusion of comfort as all of the rest surrounded her in an intimate web.

She managed to answer his question. "Yes. I didn't want to wake you but I have to shower or we'll be late meeting Ryan."

She couldn't believe how reluctant she was to jump into the new day and would rather stay nestled like this with Peter in the bed. She didn't know this woman she became when she was around Peter Clark. His effect on her was confusing, mind-boggling and scary.

With the intention of changing the image he must have gotten of her from last night, she slid

away from his arm, from his long body, from
the consolation he'd given her, quickly sat up
and combed her fingers through her hair. She
knew she looked a mess. Only her brothers had
ever seen her this early in the morning.

"About last night," she began, not knowing
exactly what to say. "That wasn't me."

Now he leisurely propped up on one elbow
and gave her a smile. "Not you? Are you telling me I just spent the night with a clone of the
real Violet Fortune?"

Feeling her cheeks pinken, she explained, "I
don't overreact. I don't get emotional. Not when
it's about medicine and doctors and patients."

His smile faded now as he pushed himself
up and sat next to her. "Last night wasn't about
medicine and doctors and patients. It was about
you caring about Ryan and what his condition
will mean to him and his family." Peter studied
her. "We wear protective shells to help us get
through each day. Last night, yours cracked."

Although he understood it all so well, she
couldn't imagine his shell ever cracking. "It's
never cracked before. I couldn't be vulnerable
in a world where men dominate...where I'm
scrutinized ever more carefully because I'm a
woman. I don't intend to let it happen again."

"Personally or professionally?"

"I can't be weak in either area. Ryan's going to need me through this and my family is, too. When I go back to my practice in New York, I have to keep my personal feelings out of it."

"Did your personal feelings have anything to do with the advice you gave to Anne?"

"Of course not! I analyzed the risks. I considered her prognosis with and without the surgery."

"Then why are you blaming yourself for what happened?"

"Because maybe I didn't analyze carefully enough."

"Violet," Peter said with a shake of his head, "I don't believe that for a minute. You've got to let go of what happened. Our patients might think we're all-knowing, but we're not. You made the best call. That's all you could do."

"But she and her baby died," Violet murmured, her heart tearing again because of it.

"Because of the aneurysm, not because of any advice you gave."

Was the situation as black-and-white as that? Was that how Peter handled his career? In cut-and-dried terms?

"Instead of dwelling on what you can't change," Peter challenged her, "concentrate on helping me convince Ryan to seek treatment. I can't let him give up without a fight."

"He's adamant about not having treatment and I can see his point. If he's going to die, he wants to live his life the best way he can until then. Chemotherapy aside, radiation on a brain tumor will make him sick, too."

"But if he can prolong his life—"

"This isn't our decision, Peter. It's Ryan's."

"And you want him to accept this verdict without challenging it?"

"I want Ryan to be at peace with whatever decision he makes."

Peter's hand sliced through the air, dismissing that idea. "Peace doesn't have to mean giving up, and I'm going to do everything I can to convince him otherwise."

Maybe Violet didn't like the idea of Peter seeing her vulnerable. Maybe she didn't like the idea of being attracted to him even if they sat here arguing. Maybe she didn't like the idea that Peter Clark was stirring up her world when it was already stirred up too much.

Sliding away from him and off the bed, she said, "I have to get a shower."

He was standing now, too, with the king-size bed between them. "Do you always just cut out of a discussion you don't like?"

"No, I don't," she answered, her back going straight. "But obviously we disagree on this.

You think more talking will pull me over to your side. It won't."

After she picked up her cosmetics case from the dresser, she took it to the bathroom doorway. "I'll see you in the lobby at eight." Stepping into the bathroom, she closed the door.

Another minute later she heard the loud thump of the motel room door shutting. Whatever tentative bonds had formed between her and Peter, they were broken now. Part of her was sad about that, the other part was relieved.

I don't need a man, she told herself again as she undressed.

Yet as she stepped into the shower, she could still feel the imprint of Peter's arm around her. She could still remember his compassion last night. It was going to be a long drive back to Red Rock.

Violet was exhausted when she returned to the Flying Aces. There had been so much tension between her and Peter concerning the argument about Ryan...along with tension of another kind.

The access road leading to the Flying Aces was tree-lined. Live oaks and sycamores threw shade over the fence line. Miles and Clyde and Steven had bought this ranch and made it a success, raising cattle and mostly chickens. The main house was a behemoth with five bedrooms. When Violet had opted to stay in the pool house instead, it afforded her privacy she desperately sought since growing up with brothers.

Now as she drove around to the pool house and parked on the gravel space next to it, her thoughts veered again to Ryan. She'd followed him to the Double Crown to make sure he'd gotten there safely. He'd waved her off before he'd turned in. She knew he was a proud man who liked to be in control. She just wished he'd share what was happening to him with everyone who loved him so they could give him support.

Sunshine lent a glow to the wood siding and reflected off of the peaked tin roof of the pool house. When Violet reached the door, keys in hand, she stopped short. There was a note taped on the glass of one French door. Removing it, she opened the note and at once recognized her friend's familiar script.

Violet—
We're back! Come to the main house when you get in and we'll catch up.
The honeymoon was wonderful.
Love, Jessica

She and Jessica had been friends since child-hood. When her friend had been in danger from a stalker, Violet had suggested she stay at the Flying Aces to hide out for a while, hoping Jessica and Clyde might turn to each other. Jessica had needed a protector and Clyde had needed a caring woman. They'd fallen in love. Apparently they'd returned from their honeymoon either late last night or this morning.

As she tucked the note inside her pants pocket, Violet swiveled on her heels and made a beeline for the main house.

Hurrying around the fenced-in pool, she went to the French doors at the dining room entrance. Jessica and Clyde were sitting there having lunch. As soon as Jessica saw her, she ran to the door and opened it. Her friend looked radiant, and Violet could see that marriage agreed with her.

"Welcome back," Violet said as she hugged her.

After returning the hug, Jessica leaned away, her dark blond hair swinging over her shoulder, her blue eyes twinkling as she studied Violet. "Miles couldn't answer our questions about where you'd gone."

"Miles didn't know," she said simply.

When Jessica's look was curious, Violet gave

a little shake of her head and her friend winked. She'd gotten the message and would drop the subject.

Violet's brother Clyde, however, wasn't going to be as amenable. He stood as she came inside, and she gave him a hug, too. Her brother was six feet tall, strong as an ox and just as stubborn.

When he leaned away, his brown eyes pinned her to the spot. "Why didn't you tell Miles where you were going?"

"Because it wasn't any of his business," she answered with a smile. The answer was supposed to throw Clyde off guard, but it didn't.

"He said you left a note saying you were going out of town and that was it."

"That *was* it," Violet responded lightly. She didn't like keeping secrets from her brothers, but she had to keep Ryan's confidence.

"Where did you go?"

If she didn't shut him down, Clyde was going to pursue this. "I had business in Houston."

"What kind of business?"

Jessica sidled over to her new husband and tucked her arm into his. "Why don't we all sit down and have some lunch."

"Violet?" Clyde prompted.

"I have a life, brother dear, that's separate from yours. Don't treat me like I'm sixteen."

A look came into Clyde's eyes then and she knew he was remembering what had happened to her when she was a teenager.

"Did you go alone?" he asked.

Violet shook her head in exasperation. "If you don't stop the third degree, I'm going back to the pool house and I'll talk with Jessica later and ignore you."

With a frown, Clyde ran a hand through his brown hair. "All right. But while you're staying here, you're my responsibility."

"I'm my *own* responsibility. I'm used to the streets of New York. You think I can't handle myself in Red Rock or in Houston?"

"I just like to know what you're up to," he grumbled, then as she and Jessica sat at the table, he did, too.

Jessica motioned to the third place she'd set. "I was hoping you'd come back and join us. Fortunately Miles stopped at a deli yesterday and brought us enough food to last for a few days."

When Violet glanced at her brother's thick sandwich, she saw it was half-eaten. Taking a piece of wheat bread from the basket on the table, she quickly made half a sandwich. "So tell me about your honeymoon."

Clyde and Jessica exchanged a look that was private and intimate, and Violet felt like an outsider. What would it be like to have that kind of connection and that kind of bond with a man? She thought about Peter and how he'd held her last night.

With a flush creeping into her cheeks, Jessica took a bite of fruit salad. "The honeymoon was wonderful."

"You should go to Cancun sometime," Clyde advised her, trying to hide a smile. Then as if he couldn't resist touching his wife a moment longer, he reached across the table and took Jessica's hand.

"I think you two could have gone anywhere and it would have been wonderful."

The newlyweds didn't disagree.

"Speaking of trips, do you still have plans to go to Italy for a shoot?"

"It will be a short one. In fact, I think Clyde might go along." Jessica grinned at her husband hopefully.

"Yes, I might." He squeezed her hand with a gentle smile. "If Miles will agree to hold down the fort again."

"What about your contract?" Violet asked, curious as to what Jessica would do with her career now that she was married.

"My work will be part-time. As a spokesperson for my company, I can still be home most of the time."

The rest of the lunch went quickly as Clyde and Jessica told her about the sights they'd seen. After Clyde downed a glass of milk and two pieces of chocolate cake, he stood and said he'd told Miles he'd check out a few things in the egg barn.

Leaning down to Jessica, he kissed her then went to the French doors. To Violet, he said, "You let me know if you're planning any more out-of-town trips."

"So you can tail me?" she asked wickedly.

Unable to suppress a grin, Clyde rolled his eyes and went outside. His quick stride took him away from the house.

Jessica said quietly, "He's worried about you, you know."

"He doesn't have any reason to worry."

"Whether you want to admit it or not, you weren't in a good place when you arrived. Are you still blaming yourself for the death of your patient?"

Jessica was the one person Violet could confide in. "I don't know. I've been trying to sort through it. It's not weighing me down quite as much."

"Do you know when you're going back to your practice?"

Shaking her head, Violet realized a lot depended on Ryan and what was going to happen with him. "Not yet."

"Miles told us you did some bidding at the bachelor auction. You bought a date with Peter Clark."

Violet groaned. "Is my life all my brothers have to talk about?"

"No, they talk about egg production and feed for the chickens and enlarging their roosting barn," Jessica told her with a grin. "But even I have to admit, you bidding on the neurosurgeon is a lot more interesting. I didn't even know you knew him. Or did you just look up at him while he was on the block, your gazes met, and poof, you outbid every woman in the room?"

Not sure how to handle this one, Violet treaded carefully. "I met Peter and somehow I got caught up in the whole auction and a donation and it just happened." That was true enough.

"When are you seeing him?"

Thinking about her argument with Peter, she knew they might not be going on the date. "I'm not sure. You know doctors and their schedules. It might never happen."

"Do you want it to happen?"

Since Violet wasn't good at subterfuge, she answered honestly. "Even if we go on a date, nothing can come of it. He's here, and I'll be returning to New York."

"It sounds as if you've thought about more than just a date."

Suddenly Violet realized how much she'd given away. Silence seemed to be her best course.

"If he's caught your attention, he must be pretty special. I know you. You'd rather read medical journals than date."

"He *is* special," Violet agreed, giving her friend that much. "He has a patient he took me to meet." She explained about Celeste.

"Are you going to see her again?"

"Yes, this evening, I hope. Tomorrow's her surgery and she's probably scared to death. I hate to think of her lying up there all alone. You should see her, Jess. She's got these big brown eyes that just melt my heart."

"I'm sure any time you spend with her will be good for her."

"I think any time I spend with her will be good for *me*."

When Violet looked up at her friend, Jessica's eyes held questions that she didn't ask. Violet was glad because she certainly didn't have any answers.

* * *

Later that day at the nurses' desk, Violet checked on Celeste's condition. Unlike Friday night, the hospital was bustling with activity as visitors came and went, and nurses cared for patients. Although she wasn't familiar with San Juan Hospital, Violet felt at home here as she did in most hospitals.

After she peered through the glass doors at Celeste, she went inside. The TV was turned on to a cartoon channel. However, Violet got Celeste's full attention as she came to sit beside her bed. "Hi, there."

"You came back," the little girl said, her words slurring a bit.

"I told you I would." She took Celeste's hand. "Tomorrow, Dr. Clark is going to start to make you better."

Celeste nodded. "He said he is. He read me a story."

"Today?"

The little girl wrinkled her brow, then nodded. "Before the nurse turned on the cartoons. I get tired of them."

"I bet you do. Would you like me to read you a story?"

Celeste's smile was wide as she said, "The one with the rainbow."

Several books lay on the serving table at the foot of the bed. Violet shuffled through them until she found the rainbow book, then sat beside Celeste and began to read.

Her fifteen minutes were almost up when Peter stepped into the cubicle. He took in the sight of her, the raspberry-colored sweater and slacks, the way she was holding Celeste's hand.

But then his attention was all for Celeste. "How's my favorite patient?"

"Okay. Violet read me a book."

"I see. I came in to tell you we're going to wake you up very early tomorrow morning so we can fix your back."

"Then I can get out of bed?"

Peter frowned. "Not tomorrow, maybe not the next day, either. But your back will start healing and someday soon you'll be out of bed and walking."

Violet checked her watch. "I know my time's up." Leaning over Celeste, she brushed the little girl's hair from her brow. "I'm going to hang around the hospital and come back in a little while. Then we can read another story or watch TV together, whatever you want to do."

"Will you come tomorrow?" Celeste asked.

The little girl touched Violet deeply. She needed someone to befriend her besides Peter.

She needed a woman's touch and Violet could give that to her. "You're going to go to sleep while Dr. Peter works on your back. I'll be here when you wake up."

"Promise?"

"I promise, and I promise I'll be back in a little while." Then unable to help herself, she gave Celeste a light kiss on the forehead, avoided Peter's gaze and slipped out the door.

Deciding not to wait to talk to him—she didn't need that turmoil right now—she headed for the elevator. She was walking down the corridor when he came up beside her and clasped her arm. His touch on her sleeve sent tingles through her body, and when she met his gaze, her pulse raced erratically until she thought about his small patient.

"Is something wrong?"

His face was as unreadable as his eyes. He was dressed casually this evening in jeans and an oxford shirt with the sleeves rolled up his arms as if he were any other visitor to the hospital. But he wasn't just any visitor.

Now he said, "Her surgery could take a while tomorrow. She might not be ready for a visitor until tomorrow evening."

"She might not be ready for a visitor but I think it's important that someone be here for her. Even if she's not awake, I think she'll sense my presence."

"You could be waiting for hours to see her."

"Then I guess I'll wait. What time is her surgery?"

"It's scheduled for eight."

"Can I see her before she goes to the operating room?"

He looked disconcerted. "I suppose you can. When I spoke to her social worker, she said she couldn't possibly get in here at that hour."

"All right. Then I'll be here at seven and I won't get in anybody's way. I just want her to know she's not alone."

His expression seemed to soften a bit. "You never do or say what I expect you to," he admitted truthfully.

"I don't know what you mean."

"Before you came to Red Rock, I formed an impression of you from Ryan, Lily, your brothers…from professional gossip."

She knew the hospital grapevines could spread around the world but she was always surprised when they did.

"You have a reputation, Dr. Fortune, as a brilliant diagnostician. The gossip highway in Red Rock has it that as the only girl in your family besides your mom—" He stopped as though he thought better of what he was going to say.

"Yes?" she prompted with a drawl.

"Never mind. I shouldn't have brought it up."

"But you did and I can guess. My family had money. I was the only girl. Therefore, I must have been spoiled, pampered, always used to getting my own way. Does that about sum it up?"

With a look of chagrin, he took a step closer to her. "Being a Fortune isn't always what it's cracked up to be, is it?"

Seeing he was sincere and maybe even understood, she gave a little shrug. "It has more advantages than disadvantages. The truth is I probably was pampered and spoiled. Still, being the only girl, I was also lonely. That's why I can understand a little how Celeste feels."

They were standing close now and she could remember everything about their night together, his gentleness and compassion, his strong arms around her, the scent of him, his body's arousal that he'd restrained and ignored.

As his gaze fell to her lips, her limbs felt weak. Then he backed away and she took a deep breath.

"If you're going to be here tomorrow, I'll try to find you after surgery and tell you how everything went," he said evenly.

"I'll be in the lounge," she responded, gesturing down the hall to the waiting room.

When he turned to leave, she added, "Peter, I'll be praying everything goes well."

He nodded and then walked away.

When Violet stepped into the elevator and the doors closed, she leaned against the back wall. Peter Clark definitely shook up her world and she had to decide if she was going to let him in or keep him out.

Right now it was a toss-up.

Chapter 6

After the night in Houston when Peter had held Violet in his arms, he'd made a decision. He had to stop whatever was happening between them and stop it fast. More than once he'd told himself physical satisfaction was fleeting. Although he knew in his gut that he and Violet would be good together, he also knew they'd get burned badly. She was exactly the type of woman he didn't date. Her life was a product of her career, as was his. Mix long distance into the recipe and they'd both be headed for disaster. People their age were set in their ways. Change could happen, but it was damn hard.

He wanted a woman who put him, home and family first.

All that resolved, he still felt as if someone had kicked him in the gut when he saw Violet with Celeste early Monday morning before the six-year-old's surgery. She was leaning over the little girl, comforting her, holding her hand. Thankful he didn't have time for conversation, he simply told Violet he'd let her know when Celeste's surgery was over.

Three hours later, he half expected her to be gone. But there she was, standing in the hospital lounge, looking out the window. Her profile was so purely feminine, her hair so damn shiny, her chin so assertive yet vulnerable at the same time, he took a deep breath and stayed put in the doorway.

"Violet," he said in an even tone.

She swung around, her face expectant.

"The fusion went well. Celeste's prognosis will depend on how determined she is to get better. She'll be in recovery for the next two hours and back up to ICU for tonight. We're hoping to move her to a regular room tomorrow."

If he'd wanted to keep a distance from Violet, he couldn't because she hurried toward him, her face bright, her eyes filled with gratitude. "While I'm here, I'll help her get better. She needs somebody to champion her...besides you."

"She *will* need support to walk again," he agreed. "Rehab is tough, but kids are usually resilient." He stopped, not wanting to prolong their conversation, but needing to cover two other points. "Have you heard from Ryan?"

"No, not a word. I wanted to give him a little time. But I'm worried about him. I'll call him this afternoon on his cell phone."

"I'm going to invite him to lunch or dinner or something and we're going to discuss treatments. He can't look at this as hopeless. Not yet."

By the expression on Violet's face, he saw she was struggling with her own feelings on the subject. Although she might strongly want Ryan to look for treatment, she would respect his decision, no matter what it was.

Peter couldn't do that. He simply couldn't. He didn't know how *not* to fight, and he was going to try to instill some of that fighting spirit into Ryan. Violet's experience with patients was apparently different from his. Maybe that was because as a surgeon, he was active in his treatment. She often had to sit by and watch nature take its course. Not an easy thing to do.

Still aware that every fiber of his being wanted to be close to her, wanted to take her into his arms, wanted to do a hell of a lot more than that, he came to the next topic for discussion.

In the matter of dates and being smooth about them, he simply wasn't. "I was going over my schedule for the weekend," he began. "You bought a date for the Riverwalk. So do you still want to do that?"

After a long look into his eyes, she responded, "If you do."

Great. She was leaving the ball in his court. "I don't break commitments I've made," he assured her. "I won't be on call on Saturday. How about Saturday night around seven?"

"Saturday night sounds good."

She sounded as if she might be looking forward to it. To his chagrin, so was he.

Her husband was avoiding her.

Lily had been sitting in the living room, reading, when Ryan came in from the barn Tuesday afternoon. His gaze had wavered from hers as he'd told her he was going upstairs to change for a business appointment in San Antonio.

Throwing her magazine on the coffee table, she felt anger rise in her all over again. Business appointment. He had too many of those. Her eyes filled with tears as she thought about Melissa Wilkes hanging all over Ryan at the bachelor auction. Married or not, that girl had her cap set for her husband. It wasn't going to happen.

A little voice inside Lily's head murmured, *Maybe it already has.*

After her reunion with Ryan and their marriage, they'd been closer than they'd ever been in their younger years. But over the past few weeks, he'd become remote, and she didn't know what to do. She'd asked him if something was wrong but as she suspected, he'd insisted there was nothing bothering him. His actions said differently. She wasn't the type of woman to just sit around and let an affair happen.

When Ryan returned to the living room, she asked, "Will you be back for dinner?"

He headed for the front door. "I doubt it. You go ahead without me. I'll see you when I get back."

A few moments later, Lily heard the heavy front door close.

He'd see her when he got back? After being with someone else? After showing his real feelings to another woman? He hadn't even given her a chance to kiss him goodbye. There was something wrong, whether he would admit it or not.

Pushing aside the magazine she'd been reading, Lily headed for the table in the foyer where she'd left her purse, hurried to the back entrance and ran to the garage. She waited outside by the side of the building until she heard Ryan start up his truck and pull out. Then she went inside the garage into her own SUV, made herself count to twenty and followed him.

As Lily tailed him, Ryan drove to San Antonio—to the east side. She almost lost him a few times, but he was traveling at a steady pace and she found his truck again. Her heart pounded along with the revolution of the tires. As instinct told her he wasn't keeping a business appointment, she hoped she was being paranoid.

Eventually Lily ended up in a development of homes. They were spacious houses with expansive properties. Lagging behind so as not to be noticed, she almost lost her husband as he turned right and then left. Finally, with his turn signal blinking, he drove into a curved, brick-patterned driveway that led to a beautiful two-story brick home.

Lily pulled up across the street under the cover and shade of tall trees and quickly opened her glove compartment, removing small binoculars she used on the ranch to spot wildlife. Now she focused them on the arched doorway of the home. As she feared, a woman opened the door—a woman who appeared to be in her early thirties, a woman with long, straight blond hair, a woman who was very sleek in jeans and very beautiful though in Lily's estimation very pale. To Lily's horror and dismay, she not only saw a woman at the door, but a boy with blond bangs who looked to be about ten. He was wearing a soccer uniform and smiling. Ryan enveloped him in a huge hug.

That was all Lily needed to see. Tears welled up in her eyes and she felt as if she couldn't catch her breath. The door of the house closed, and she sat there stunned.

When she felt her tears on her hands, she knew she had to drive away. She knew she had to go back to the Double Crown and figure out what she was going to do.

As she switched on the ignition, thoughts and feelings raced through her so fast she couldn't catch hold of them. All she knew was that her heart hurt and nothing would ever be the same again.

The Riverwalk was a San Antonio experience and a happening place, especially on a

Saturday night. In a casual blouse and slacks, Violet strolled beside Peter wishing away the awkwardness between them. When he'd picked her up at the pool house, she'd caught a glimpse of Miles watching her from the back of the big house. Both he and Clyde knew this was her auction date and had teased her unmercifully. Jessica, on the other hand, had wanted to know if she'd seen Peter at the hospital when she returned from visiting Celeste.

The truth was, Violet hadn't seen Peter since the afternoon after Celeste's surgery. He couldn't be avoiding her because she never went to the hospital at exactly the same time. Yet tonight they seemed to have a wall between them and she didn't know how to tear it down.

"It's a nice night," he commented, breaking the silence as they strolled along the gray cobblestone path.

The aroma of grilled onions and steaks, fried seafood and garlic filled the air along with the sound of the horn from a flatbed water taxi, people talking, the drone of a plane overhead.

Violet glanced at Peter. He looked handsome and strong and virile in khaki slacks, and a black-and-tan-striped Henley shirt. "It would be nicer if I didn't feel as if I were on a forced date with you," she said honestly, hoping to clear the air.

Stopping, he looked at her and a wry smile tilted his lips. "Aah. I thought I was the only one feeling that."

"I wanted to come tonight, Peter. I just wish we could be friends instead of…opponents. We should be on the same side, not different ones."

After a long, silent moment, he said, "I found a hospital in New York City that has openings in its clinical trials. If Ryan qualifies, he could get a spot."

"And if he doesn't *want* to qualify?" she challenged him.

There was a bench under one of the oaks. Peter took her arm and led her in that direction, sitting down beside her. "I mean to convince him to look at possibilities."

"Sometimes even doctors have to bow to the inevitable."

"Maybe so. But I can tell you, even an extra week is important to loved ones who are left behind."

That opened the door and Violet walked in. "Your family was left by your mother. Is that why you're so determined?"

"You're damned straight, that's why. My mother was the personification of a life well lived. She couldn't do enough for others. Her family came first, including the foster kids, but that wasn't all. She volunteered at the thrift shop and helped in the soup kitchen. In the world's terms, I guess she wasn't successful, but in humanitarian terms, she was damn near perfect."

"What happened to her?"

"It doesn't matter," Peter muttered, looking across the walk at a storefront.

"I think it does." She rested her hand on his arm. "Please tell me."

His gaze returned to hers then and something passed between them—something she could feel deep down inside, something she'd never felt before in talking to a man. Removing her hand from his arm, she placed it in her lap and waited.

"She had a couple of dizzy spells. The doctors prescribed tests and we learned she had a brain tumor. Three months later, she was gone. The explanation that she'd gone to heaven just didn't cut it. We were still trying to wrap our minds around that when less than a year later Dad remarried."

"That *was* fast." Violet could hear the flat disapproval that she sensed Peter was trying to let go of.

"It was too fast for me. Linda and Stacey seemed to cope better, maybe because they were girls and needed a mother. I didn't need a replacement. I needed to keep the memories alive of the one I'd had. By marrying that quickly, Dad seemed to be making a statement that life moved on and Mom hadn't been important."

"I'm sure he didn't feel that way."

"No. He and I talked about it later. Before I went to college, we had one of those father-son chats that both guys dread. He talked a lot more than I did. I guess he sensed that I might go off and not come back."

"Could that have happened?"

Now Peter studied the people strolling along the Riverwalk. "No. I cared about Stacey and Linda and the other kids too much. And I did love my father. I just hadn't agreed with what he'd done. He explained that Charlene had come along at just the right time. He admitted that after Mom died, he felt totally lost and out of his depth and he needed someone to help with all of us. We had two foster kids living with us—Jamie and Carla—who were both younger than Linda. Charlene stepped in and took over, but it just didn't feel right. Jamie and Carla were with us about another year—Jamie went back to his mother and Carla was actually adopted. After that, Charlene and Dad didn't take in more kids. I bet fifteen kids went through our lives when Mom was living."

"Not every woman can be a mother to all kids."

"I realized that even then. And I know Charlene stepped in with three strikes against her as far as I was concerned. But to me, she just never measured up."

"And now?"

"She's made my dad happy. She's friends with Linda and Stacey and they call her often. She and I respect each other, but we keep our distance. That's the way it's always going to be."

"And you became a neurosurgeon so patients didn't die of brain tumors."

"Something like that."

After he stood, he brought the personal conversation to an end. "Now you have the history of Peter Clark and why I believe Ryan should take a chance on living."

Rising to her feet beside him, she looked up at him. "I agree with you in theory. I do. But we aren't in Ryan's shoes and he just wants to make the most of the time he does have."

With a slight shake of his head, Peter gave

her a wry smile. "I guess if we want to enjoy tonight, we're going to have to just agree to disagree."

"I can do that," she decided.

He motioned down the Riverwalk, lined with outdoor seating and colorful umbrellas. "Good, then let me take you to my favorite restaurant. It serves the best pasta-and-lobster dish I've ever eaten."

An hour and a half later, Violet dabbed her mouth with her napkin after putting down her dessert fork, then smiled at Peter. "You were right. That's the best meal I've ever eaten. And the cheesecake was delicious. Do you think the chef would give me his recipes?"

Peter chuckled. "For a price."

They'd split a piece of white chocolate cheesecake, and now Violet pushed the empty plate aside. Candlelight flickered in the globe lantern on the table, and with fascination, she watched the shadows from it play on Peter's face. He wasn't just good-looking in a quiet, casual yet determined sort of way, but his face was full of character, too. It showed in the fine lines around his eyes and the set of his jaw.

Time had sifted much too quickly through the hourglass as they'd talked and laughed and eaten. She felt like Cinderella and had to remind herself that this wasn't a real date. Peter hadn't asked her here of his own free will. She'd bought the pleasure of his company and she'd be a fool to forget it.

A band had started playing while they were eating and couples danced on the dance floor. There wasn't much room but no one looked as if they minded.

"How about another piece of cheesecake?" Peter asked.

Violet shook her head. "No, thank you. My jeans are already getting tight. In New York I usually live on black coffee and yogurt."

"I don't think you have a thing to worry about."

Peter's compliment, as well as the look in his green eyes, sent her pulse racing. She really wasn't used to this man-woman interplay and wasn't sure how to handle it.

He took the necessity of a response out of her hands. "If not more dessert, how about a dance?"

Her pulse raced at the invitation. "I'd like that."

He rose from his wicker chair and came around the glass-topped table to lead her to the tiny dance floor.

"I'm rusty at this," he murmured as he took her into his arms.

"No rustier than I am," she admitted, thinking maybe she shouldn't have.

"No time to date and dance, or no inclination?"

How did she answer that one? "I don't need to tell you that when I have the inclination, I don't have the time. When I have the time, I'm usually too tired or have too many errands to run to have the inclination."

"Maybe you could explain that to Linda and Stacey for me. They seem to think that when Friday or Saturday night arrives and I'm not on call, I should be painting the town red. I can't seem to get through to them that a night at home alone is a good thing."

"Do you want more?" Violet suddenly wanted to know.

"Eventually. Someday. With the right person."

"How are you going to know?" she asked and swallowed hard. It seemed to be such an important question.

"I'll just know."

Everyone thought that and the idea seemed so simple. But nothing was simple as Peter looked down at her and pulled her a little closer. Her blood ran hot and she knew her reaction to him was about more than chemistry. She suspected he did, too.

With his lips close to her temple, he said in a low voice, "If we spend time together, we're going to get into trouble."

Remembering his kiss, remembering him holding her, she knew that was true. Yet for the moment she didn't care. With so many people in such a small space, no one was paying attention to anyone else. The atmosphere around them became steamy with their thoughts and Violet wondered if Peter's were as X-rated as hers. She'd never felt this way with a man. Never.

Leaning away slightly, he gazed at her lips and she was filled with anticipation.

"Trouble," he repeated. His head lowered and his mouth pressed firmly onto hers as rockets seemed to explode in the room.

When his tongue breached her lips, the kiss became an event like standing in the middle of Times Square on New Year's Eve, like riding the rapids down the Colorado River, like flying to the moon. When his hand pressed up and down her back, she knew he could feel her bra strap, she knew he could feel her tremble, she knew if he ever made love to her she probably wouldn't recover. Then he angled the kiss differently and one of his hands slid between them, and she knew he was feeling as reckless as she was. When his thumb found her nipple through her top, her soft moan was lost in the kiss, lost in the music, lost to her and found by him. He answered it with deeper strokes of his tongue, with a more erotic caress of her breast, with the pressure of his lower body against hers.

Suddenly she wished they were anywhere else but here. Somewhere private, somewhere where they could undress each other and let their hands wander over each other's bodies. When she thought about kissing Peter other places—

His hand slid from her breast as he leaned back slightly. "Like I said. Trouble," he muttered.

She almost smiled at his chagrin, but his comment wiped her smile away.

"Do you intend to return to New York when this business with Ryan is over?" he asked.

She knew what would happen if she said no. She knew what would happen if she said yes. But she had to be honest with him. That was the only way she knew how to be. "Yes, I'll be returning to New York. My practice is there. My life is there."

"That's the way I feel about Red Rock." For a moment he rested his chin on her head. "Your career takes up most of your life," he concluded as if that wasn't a noble thing.

"Yours does, too."

"I'm not denying that, but I tried a relationship with a doctor before. Her career came first and she—"

He stopped and Violet desperately wanted to know how that woman had hurt Peter. From what he'd told her about his mother and the way he'd grown up, she already suspected that he wanted a relationship with a woman who could be devoted to him and a family. Apparently he'd found that out the hard way, just as she'd found out when she was fifteen that a woman could look for love in all the wrong places, that a woman could believe a man's desire for her could make her less lonely...could make her happy.

The song ended and she realized her date with Peter had ended, too. They didn't have anywhere to go from here. If they gave in to their attraction, they'd both get hurt...badly.

When he led her back to their table, he didn't have to say a word.

She picked up her purse while he paid their bill. They left the restaurant in silence, and for the first time in Violet's life, she wished she'd taken a different career path.

Chapter 7

Late Sunday morning when Celeste's little arms came up around Violet's neck and gave her a huge hug, Violet felt tears come to her eyes. She willed them away. She wasn't a woman prone to crying. However, in the past few weeks she couldn't seem to help herself.

Tears made her feel weak.

Every time she had to leave Celeste, her heart hurt. That was so odd because she'd never felt attached to a child in just this way before.

"Will you come back tomorrow?" Celeste asked. Her medications were being withdrawn slowly and she was more alert now.

"I'll come back tonight," Violet assured her.

"I'll bring a new book. I think we've read the ones here twenty-five times each."

"Not that many," Celeste said with a smile.

An hour later when Violet left Celeste's room, she wondered if it wouldn't be better if the six-year-old wasn't alone, if she had some company in her room. She'd have to talk to Peter about it.

Besides the private and semiprivate rooms in the pediatrics unit, there was a ward with six beds. As Violet passed it now, she heard a woman's voice reading a familiar story. She recognized the voice. It had rung loud and clear when she had put Peter up for bid at the auction.

When Violet peeked her head into the room, Stacey Clark saw her and held her finger up for Violet, signaling for her to wait.

With most of her day free, Violet didn't mind. She stood outside the room and listened. Stacey was a good storyteller. It wasn't long until Stacey finished the story, closed the book, chatted with the kids a few minutes and then came into the hall. "I didn't mean to hold you up."

"That's all right."

"How did your date go on the Riverwalk?"

That was a minefield. "The Riverwalk is beautiful at night."

Stacey tilted her head and eyed Violet

shrewdly. "That was a sidestep if ever I heard one. What did my brother *do?*"

"Your brother was a perfect gentleman." At least for most of the evening, she amended to herself.

"So that's what he did wrong!"

Violet had to laugh. "Peter was perfect. We had a wonderful dinner and even danced a little."

"Hmm. Will I get any more info if I ask *him?*"

"I doubt that," Violet answered wryly.

"You're getting to know him already." Then Stacey's expression turned serious. "I was just hoping—"

"What were you hoping?" Violet prompted.

"That you two would fall madly in love and he'd have something else in his life besides work."

Although Violet didn't know whether to find Stacey's honesty daunting or totally refreshing, it took her aback. "Don't you think he can run his own life?"

"Oh, he runs his life. On a fast track. But he doesn't have time to stop and smell the roses. The way he looked at you, I was hoping you'd sidetrack him."

"For a second, maybe," Violet admitted. "But he wants a lot more than I can give him."

After Stacey studied her for a few moments she muttered, "Peter expects too much."

"He knows what he wants—a life here in Red Rock and a woman who's all about home and hearth."

"You *do* know him already."

The past two weeks had been so strange. She and Peter hadn't been intimate. Not in the real sense of the word. However, intimacy had seemed to flow between them, whether they liked it or not. They'd been plunged into a situation where they'd gotten to know each other very quickly.

"Are you going to see him again?" At Violet's sigh, Stacey added, "I know, I know. I'm nosy and a meddler. But *are* you?"

"Probably only in conjunction with Celeste." That idea didn't please her at all.

Suddenly Stacey snapped her fingers and her face brightened with a wide smile. "I have a great idea. There's an anniversary party for my dad and his wife tonight at the community center room at the Town and Country condo complex. Why don't you come?"

"I don't know your dad or his wife. Wouldn't that seem a little strange?"

"Not at all. You know me and Linda and Peter. And I'd like you to meet them. I think you'd like my stepmother. She's involved in a cause I really believe in. And, to be a bit self-serving here, she can always use donations for it."

"What is it?"

"Why don't you come and let her tell you?"

"I don't know, Stacey."

"Look, this is how it is. Peter will probably come late and leave early. You might not even see him. We're having a buffet at seven and the party will end when it ends. Please say you'll come."

A good cause and a glimpse of Peter. "Do you need an answer right now?"

"Nope. Come if you want, stay at home if you please. If you don't come, I'll find another way to introduce you to Charlene."

Violet was curious as to why Stacey seemed to like her stepmother so much, but Peter had backed off from her. "It sounds as if you and your stepmother have a good relationship."

"Charlene's great. She filled a huge gap in our lives. It couldn't have been easy, taking over three kids that weren't hers plus two foster children, learning how to become a mom and a wife all in one fell swoop. She didn't have an easy time of it with Peter, but she never became indifferent to him, either. She was just always there."

Now Violet's curiosity was really piqued.

Stacey glanced at her watch. "I've got to get going. I told Linda I'd meet her at the community room and make sure everything was ready for tonight. I really hope you'll join us." With a grin and a final wave, Stacey went down the hall to the elevator.

Should she or shouldn't she go tonight? Did she want to see Peter again?

Yes.

Did he want to see her? That was questionable.

After she'd dressed for the evening, Violet applied lipstick. Whether she was being wise or not, she'd decided to attend the anniversary party for Charlene and George Clark. She didn't have to stay long. She might not even see Peter. But since Stacey had extended the invitation, Violet would like to accept the overture. She was also interested in whatever Charlene Clark's charity might be.

When Violet's phone rang, she capped her lipstick. Crossing to the sitting area of the pool house, she picked up her cell phone lying beside her purse. "Hello."

Patrick Fortune's deep voice boomed through the phone lines. "I want to know what my long-lost daughter has been doing for the past two weeks, since she didn't seem to have time to call me."

Violet hadn't called her family for a very good reason. If they asked about Ryan, she didn't want to lie or evade. "Do you check up on Miles, Clyde, Steven and Jack when they haven't phoned you for two weeks?"

Her father chuckled. "You always did know how to make a point. We miss you, that's all. How's it going in Red Rock?" Then he added gently, "And give me the truth, not what you think I want to hear."

Her throat tightened. Her father was a wonderful man. She hadn't seen him much as she was growing up because his work as president of Fortune-Rockwell Banking kept him away for long hours and took him on business trips. But after her rebellion at fifteen and her search for someone to love only her had left her with an ectopic pregnancy that had almost taken her life, she'd gotten to know her father better. After her emergency surgery, he'd cut back his hours and his business trips. She hadn't asked him to do that, but he'd sensed why she'd reached out to a boy with no sense of responsibility, with no idea of where he was going in the future. Through his actions, her father had proved to her that she was important to him. At that point in her life, it had mattered more than almost anything else in the world.

"There's a lot going on here," she told him now. "Ryan's under a lot of stress from the murder investigation. Steven and Amy are finalizing preparations for the awards ceremony at his ranch. I'm…in and out of all of it."

"And in your professional life?" he asked gently. "Do you still blame yourself for Anne Washburn's death?"

Her father had always been a cut-to-the-chase man. Peter had that quality, too. "In part. But I'm helping with one of Peter Clark's patients. He's a neurosurgeon here."

"Helping? You mean consulting?"

"No, not exactly. Her name is Celeste and she's six." She told him a little about the girl. "I'm spending some time with her, talking to her, reading to her. I think it's helping me as much as it's helping her."

There was a long pause, as if her father was debating about his next words. But he said them anyway. "If you want children of your own someday, you're going to have to take a few risks."

"How do you know I haven't?"

"You're afraid you're going to find the wrong relationship again. You're afraid an ectopic pregnancy will happen again. You work to fill up your life, but it's not filling up. How am I doing?"

"Too well," she murmured. "I don't consciously think all of that."

"Of course you don't, because you're an intelligent woman and you can reason your way through it. The problem is, your heart doesn't accept the reasoning."

"You should have been a psychologist instead of a financier."

He laughed. "I don't think your mother would agree with that. Sometimes she insists I'd rather live in the Dark Ages than see the light of the new millennium. And she's probably right. The Dark Ages are more restful."

Now Violet laughed with him. Her mother was a fireball—a go-getter, a forward-looking, forge-ahead kind of woman. During her childhood, Violet had seen Lacey fight for her causes—better schools, good day care, laws to protect battered women—and she'd believed that those causes came first.

Her triplet brothers had been older than Violet, involved in sports, dating and general ruckus, determined to fend for themselves like their oldest brother, Jack. Violet, feeling out-numbered by males, had turned inward and had somehow gotten lost for a while. But Lacey was the one who had found Violet when her ectopic pregnancy ruptured. Lacey had been the one who had sat by her bed hour after hour, night after night. There had been no doubt, then and after, that her mother loved her, cared about her and wanted only the best for her.

It had been her mother who'd hired a tutor and, knowing her daughter's capabilities, had exposed her to professions she'd be interested in. She'd encouraged her to become what-ever she wanted to be. Her dad was happy she loved her work. Her mother, however, was so proud when she introduced Violet as her doc-tor-daughter, that Violet never wanted to let her down.

"Are you seeing much of your brothers?" her father asked.

"Jack and Gloria are away on vacation. I had breakfast with Clyde and Jessica after they got back. They're still in newlywed heaven. Miles is either working or out on the town tonight. Rumor has it he dates a different woman every week. When I ask him about it, he just smiles, shrugs and says he's sowing his wild oats. But

I don't know if he's having as much fun as he's pretending to have. A pretty nurse bid on him at the bachelor auction and I think they had a good time on their date. But I don't think he's going to see her again."

"Did *you* bid on a bachelor at this auction?"

She hesitated a moment then answered, "Yes, I did."

"Does this bachelor have a name?"

"Actually, it's Dr. Clark, the neurosurgeon I mentioned."

"The one with the patient you're getting attached to?"

Her dad always summed things up in a nutshell. She *was* getting attached to Celeste. "Yes, that doctor."

"And?"

"And, nothing. He's not interested in a woman whose career is as demanding as his. Especially not if she's in New York."

"Hmm. I seem to remember thinking your mother was too spirited, too intense and too passionate for me to handle. But Cupid has a way of changing our minds. If he wants to shoot an arrow in your direction, maybe you should welcome it."

"You're full of advice today."

"Uh-oh. That's my cue to hang up. Don't

want to overstay my conversation. Your mother and I have been thinking about making another visit to Red Rock soon, so don't be surprised if we show up."

"No warning?"

"That depends."

"I love you, Dad," she said.

"I love you, too, baby. See you soon."

If she'd had doubts about attending this anniversary party for Peter's parents before her father called, she didn't have them now. She was going to take a risk, even if it wasn't a very big one.

Peter was late.

He'd gotten tied up at the hospital. As he looked back over the afternoon and the crisis with one of his patients, he hoped his father and stepmother didn't look at his lateness as a slight. He had a decent relationship with them both now, and he didn't want to spoil that.

Their condo was part of a complex that was like a village. It even had a small convenience store. The community room was used for square dances and bingo and Tupperware parties. Now it was festively decorated with an anniversary banner and helium-filled balloons. The buffet table was long and still full.

His gaze unerringly found his dad and step-mother, along with his sisters. When he saw who was with them, he stopped short. What was Violet doing here?

Stacey saw him and beckoned him over. His brows rose as he looked at Violet and she pinkened a little. Telling himself her presence didn't matter, he congratulated his father and stepmother and wished them many more years together.

After Charlene studied him, she asked, "Do you mean that?"

"Very much. You've made my dad happy. After he retires, you can do things together you've never had time to do. Maybe take that Grecian cruise."

"That's what I got her for our anniversary," his father said with a laugh. "No time like the present. Who knows what will happen in five years? We're going to enjoy ourselves now."

Peter knew he looked like his dad, though his father was now mostly gray, wore bifocals that sat high on his nose and seemed uncomfortable in his suit.

As Charlene slipped her hand into his dad's, she smiled. She was a striking woman, with ash-blond hair, green eyes and a figure she worked hard to preserve. Now she nodded to

Stacey, Linda and Violet. "Violet, you know Peter, don't you?"

Deciding to keep the atmosphere light, he explained, "She's helping me with one of my patients."

"And," Linda interjected, "Violet bid on Peter at the bachelor auction. They went to the Riverwalk Saturday night."

Now he was just as uncomfortable as Violet looked.

Plowing ahead with the conversation, Charlene explained, "I was just describing my home for unwed mothers that's been renovated. We hope to start operations next month." She suggested to Violet, "If you have time, you should come and look around. I'll explain what we're going to do there."

Meaning it as a joke, Peter said to Violet, "She probably would like a donation to the endowment fund."

As soon as he said it, he saw the hurt look in Charlene's eyes, but she didn't make a comeback or contradict him.

With a frown at Peter, Linda said to both Charlene and her father, "I see the Wilsons over there. They're looking your way. I think they'd like to talk to you. Come on, let's make the rounds."

As the group walked away, Violet was left standing there with him.

"I stepped in it again," he said with a sigh. When Violet remained quiet, he asked, "What do you think of Charlene?"

"I only spoke with her a few minutes. We were comparing notes on renovating old houses. I remembered my parents doing that when I was a child."

"Before your dad could buy any house he wanted in the universe?"

"Way before that. I think I was three. There are pictures in the family album of me wielding a paintbrush and getting more on me than on the wall."

Again, that awkwardness overtook them— the awkwardness that comes after a deep, explosive, passionate kiss, when both people don't know what to do or say.

Now he asked the first thing that came into his head. "Why did you come tonight?"

"After I visited Celeste this afternoon, I ran into Stacey. We started talking and she invited me. But now I realize I shouldn't have come."

"Why not?" He was as interested in her answer as her reasons for coming.

"Because twice now I've put you in an awkward situation. At the auction and now here. I enjoy your company and you're a great listener, but I won't force my presence on you again. I do want to know how Ryan reacts to the idea of an experimental program, but I'll find that out from him."

Then before he could even think about what to say to all of that, she murmured good-night and headed for his parents to say her goodbyes.

Peter was never confused. He always saw his course clearly with a patient. He never vacillated once he made a decision, either in his professional or personal life. But Violet Fortune confused the hell out of him. As his libido told him not to let her walk out of the community room door, his head told him that was the best thing for both of them. He went with his head.

It wasn't until he glanced at his bedside clock at 2:00 a.m. that he realized his decision had been a bad one. Violet Fortune made him smile. She made him laugh. Most of all, she made him need. It was the needing that unsettled him most. What would happen if they did spend more time together?

As he punched his pillow, repositioned it and lay back on it again, he decided to find out.

When Peter drove to the Flying Aces the following afternoon, he had a plan, knowing full well it could go up in smoke if Violet wasn't at the pool house. He'd considered the hand fate was going to have in this. He wasn't the type of man to let fate decide anything for him, if he could help it. But in this instance, kismet could be the deciding factor.

He'd been to the Flying Aces before. As he took the access road, it veered toward the main house. Since the pool house was in the back, he headed his SUV for the lane that went in that direction. To his surprise, he felt relief when he saw Violet's car. He pulled up in back of it, parked and went to the door of the pool house. She could be anywhere, he told himself.

He raised his closed hand to knock, but before he could, the door opened and Violet stood there, looking as if she'd just stepped from the pages of a rodeo magazine in a red-and-white checked blouse, jeans and boots.

She gazed up at him with concerned blue eyes. "Peter! What are you doing here? Has something happened to Ryan? Celeste?"

"No. Nothing like that. I came for another reason, though it does have something to do with Celeste."

"Has her social worker found her a family?"

"No. I have to choose a rehab facility for her. There are two I have in mind, and I thought maybe you'd like to go along and look them over with me."

"Now?"

"Yes. One of my partners is covering for me for the afternoon and evening. Are you busy?"

"I was going to go riding, but that can wait. I just have to get my purse, then I'll be ready."

On the drive to San Antonio, feeling pleased he'd managed to snag Violet, he filled the silence by telling her about both facilities. "We'll visit Tumbleweed Terrace Rehab Hospital first and then drive to Lonestar Rehab."

At Tumbleweed, Violet went through the paces with Peter, meeting the director, dropping into occupational therapy rooms as well as physical therapy activities, observing the children and young adults who made up the majority of the patients. When she peeked into the area of the facility that housed whirlpools, aqua-massage and showers, she looked thoughtful. At the pool she spoke to a therapist who was putting away equipment and asked questions about individual and group therapy. They spoke for a few moments with a counselor who guided all of the patients who were admitted.

The second facility, a ten-minute drive from the first, was much different in its decor as well as its atmosphere. Definitely more clinical, it had no murals of Disney characters on the walls. The hospital, however, had a staff that was just as dedicated. The general population of patients was made up of a smattering of all ages, with a high concentration of the elderly.

When they left Lonestar and climbed into Peter's SUV, Violet turned to him. "I think you've already made up your mind, haven't you?"

Nothing he'd said could have given her that impression. "I know which one I'd send her to. I want your opinion."

"She'll be better suited to Tumbleweed. I have no doubt everyone at Lonestar would be solicitous, forward-looking, and would take her under their wing…"

"But?"

"But Celeste needs to be around children. She's alone and lonely and needs to bond with kids her own age if she can. So I have to wonder again why you asked me to come along."

She was looking at him as if she expected the whole truth and nothing but the truth. "I *did* want your opinion," he maintained. "I'm not completely objective when it comes to Celeste. At Tumbleweed not all of the therapies would be covered, but I don't want that to play into this choice. If I send her there, I'll subsidize whatever's necessary."

Violet waited.

So much for the diplomatic answer. "There was another reason I asked you to come along. I didn't like the way you left the anniversary party."

After a moment of silence, she admitted, "I didn't feel as if I belonged there."

"I made you feel that way?"

"You didn't want me there."

Already he knew Violet was a straight shooter. However, her honesty made him face facts squarely. "From the moment we met, you and I...connected. It was a shock to me."

"I know what you mean."

The smile trembling on her lips made him want to kiss her. Instead, he reached over and took her hand. "The problem with you being at that anniversary party was that I wanted you there too much. After the Riverwalk I decided that we needed to put a tight lid on what we were feeling. Especially put a lid on the desire that churns up whenever we get within a foot of each other."

Her eyes were bluer and very serious as she asked, "Have you changed your mind?"

"Have you?" he challenged her, gently.

"I'm here, aren't I?"

"Because of Celeste."

"Because of Celeste. *And* because of you."

His blood was rushing faster. "We're headed down a dangerous road."

"We can put on the brakes anytime we want," she insisted.

Unable to resist, he leaned over to her and kissed her. It was a hard kiss. A hungry kiss. A short kiss. But its brevity didn't dilute its effect.

When he broke it off, he cleared his throat and asked, "You really think we can put on the brakes?"

Wide-eyed, she nodded.

"We have to be damn sure we both want what's going to happen." After a quick glance at her, he suggested, "Let's go see Celeste and tell her where she'll be going to get better."

Maybe as they put the child first, he'd convince himself getting involved with Violet Fortune wasn't an insanely stupid thing to do.

Chapter 8

Peter's desire for Violet was getting harder to handle. Not acting on it was giving him sleepless nights. Unable to get a good read on her, he wondered if she felt hostage to the chemistry, too. After all, neither of them wanted to get hurt. Neither of them wanted to complicate their lives more than necessary. Yet whatever was growing between them was getting too hot to handle.

Peter felt like taking her hand as they walked down the hall to pediatrics, and that was absolutely irrational. He'd never considered himself the hand-holding type!

When Violet glanced at him right before they

stepped into Celeste's room, the look in her eyes urged him to draw her into his arms. But that was out of the question here.

Celeste's bed was tilted up. Her physical therapist had told Peter she was responding to therapy and she'd do well in rehab. He hoped that was true. He didn't want her having a setback. The nurse on duty had told him Violet had been in to see Celeste this morning and had stayed a couple of hours. He guessed Violet's visits had a lot to do with Celeste's cooperation with the therapist.

Now as Violet went to the child, he could feel the affection between them. It was obvious Celeste looked up to Violet, and he could see Violet's deep caring for his patient.

Sitting beside Celeste, Violet took her hand. "Hi, sweetie. I told you I'd be back. How'd today go?"

"They moved my legs."

"You mean the therapist exercised them?" Celeste nodded.

"It hurt," she said with a small pout.

"A lot?"

"No, not a lot. But I want it to stop hurting."

"I know you do." Violet's gaze went to Peter, and he gave a nod.

"We know you're probably tired of the hospital, so we made arrangements for you to go someplace where you'll get better faster," she explained.

"What place?"

Stepping forward then, Peter explained, "It's called Tumbleweed Terrace. It's sort of like a hospital, but better because there will be other kids there."

"Like me?"

Celeste was bright and grasped more than Peter expected. "Some are like you. Some have different problems. But everybody's trying to get well."

Suddenly she looked scared. "Will you go with me?"

After Peter crossed to where Violet was seated, he put his hand on Celeste's shoulder. "We can't go with you, but we can visit."

Without warning, Celeste reached her arms out to Violet, and instinctively Violet seemed to know what to do. Hopping up onto the bed, she lay beside Celeste and tucked her arm around her shoulders, holding her as close as she could. "It'll be all right, honey. Really, it will. I went with Dr. Clark to meet the people at Tumbleweed who will be taking care of you. They're all very nice."

"I want *you* to be there."

Smoothing the little girl's hair, Violet murmured, "I'll visit you as much as I can. I promise. You're going to be so busy, you might not even want me to visit."

Vigorously shaking her head, Celeste repeated, "I want you there."

"I'm going to visit, too," Peter assured her. "Tumbleweed isn't so very far away from here, only about five minutes. So I can come have lunch with you, or a snack, or read you a story."

"Do you like *The Little Mermaid?*" Violet asked.

Winding her hair around one finger—Violet had noticed Celeste did that when upset—the girl nodded.

"Good. Because Ariel's painted on one of the walls in the hall. Really big. I also saw some dogs with spots."

Celeste giggled. "Lots of doggies."

Even Peter knew they were referring to *101 Dalmatians*.

"Can you read me a story?" she asked.

Violet turned to Peter. "Is that a problem?"

With a shrug, he answered, "Not at all."

Bending over Celeste, he ruffled her hair. "They have a whole lot more books at Tumbleweed, too. Maybe we can find new stories to read."

Celeste still didn't look sure about the whole thing, he thought as he pulled up a bedside chair. Change was hard at any age, and Celeste had had much too much of it.

When Peter drove Violet back to the Flying Aces that evening, he wasn't ready to let her go.

Maybe she was feeling the same way because she asked, "Would you like to come in? I'm not much of a cook, but I can make an omelet."

The full moon shining down on the hood of the car gave him an idea. "Do you ever go riding at night?"

"Once in a while. But I don't like doing it alone. Both Miles and Clyde get up before dawn so I haven't asked them to go along. And Jessica, being a newlywed and all…" Her voice trailed off and she gave a little laugh.

"I haven't been on a night ride in years. Are you interested in doing it tonight?" If he'd had a better turn of phrase he would have used it.

In the moonlight he could see the smile on Violet's lips from the double entendre. "I think a night ride would be wonderful."

"Good. Then let's go saddle up."

Once inside the barn, Violet introduced him to a few of the mounts and told him to pick one. He selected a pewter-gray horse named Stormy.

As Violet rubbed the gelding's nose, she said, "His name has to do with his color, not his disposition. He's a great trail horse."

"Which one's yours?"

"How did you know I had one?"

"My guess is your brothers had a horse just for you the first time you came to the ranch."

She laughed again, and he so liked the sound of it. "You're right about that," she told him, pointing to a chestnut mare with a black mane. "Her name's Dixie, and I love her." With an appraising look at Peter's feet clad in sneakers, she decided, "I bet you can fit into a pair of Miles's boots. He keeps a spare pair in the tack room. Come on."

Fifteen minutes later they led their horses into the corral and mounted them under the moon and starlit sky. All afternoon Peter had been admiring the fit of Violet's jeans. She'd grabbed a flannel jacket from the barn to put on over her blouse, but as she mounted, he admired her long legs and slim figure all over again. Unable to control his body's reaction, he allowed his thoughts to take him to a bed with her in it.

They were able to ride side by side on the well-worn trail. The leaves of pecan trees rustled against each other in the breeze. Their horses's hooves clip-clopped along on the packed earth as an owl gave out a long, drawn-out hoot. All around them, moonlight spilled across the landscape, glimmering on the roof of an out-building, spreading streams of light through wispy tree branches, delineating the trail they were taking.

When they reached a fork, Violet led them to the right. "There's a lake this way. It's safe to pick up speed for a while."

His horse moved into a canter first, and then hers followed. With the night breeze in his hair, with the power of a horse under him, with Violet beside him, he felt suddenly free of burdens...free of the responsibility of being a neurosurgeon...free of the shackles that often led his sisters to poke fun at him. For a while now he'd considered his relationship with Sandra Mason to have been a thing of the past, to have been over and done with. But since he'd met Violet, what had happened then had affected now. Violet wasn't Sandra. Yet her career and where she practiced could be obstacles in their path.

Now, however, he saw no obstacles as they rode toward the lake. Moonlight lit their world, and darkness and silence created an intimacy he craved with Violet.

Nearing the lake, she slowed her mount to a walk again and so did he. There was something dreamlike about the silver water stretching before them, the trees and brush creating dark shadows that could envelop them if not for the moon. A light mist hovering over the water seemed almost magical. The scents of leaves and moss and Violet's perfume all belonged together...right here, right now.

"Do you want to dismount?" Peter asked.

"If we do, I'm afraid it'll disappear."

He wasn't a romantic. He wasn't a mystic. But at that moment, he knew exactly what she meant. "Let's prove it's real," he suggested.

They tethered their horses to brush damp with evening moisture. Then Peter did what he'd wanted to do that afternoon. He took Violet's hand, and they found a narrow path leading to the edge of the lake.

After he stopped where the brush thickened, he dropped an arm around her shoulders. "Warm enough?" he asked.

"I am now."

When she angled her body to face his and looked up at him, her eyes sparkled.

Nothing on this earth could have kept him from kissing her. Everything about Violet Fortune was deep and thrilling and altogether enticing. She fit into his arms as if she were made for him. When his hands laced in her soft, silky hair, he pressed his body against hers, fitting them together intimately.

There was no hesitancy on her part as her arms went around his neck and she murmured, "What changed your mind?"

He knew what she meant. When he'd come to the Flying Aces today, he'd decided to push a little further with Violet, to explore a little deeper. Right or wrong, wise or not. "I kept trying to talk myself out of it. But every time I saw you—"

"What?"

"I wanted to do this." Bringing her mouth to his, he crushed her lips with his.

It had been too long since the last kiss. During that time, there had been too many dreams and not enough reality. This kiss was as real as they got. When his tongue pushed into her mouth, she not only accepted his invasion, but responded to it. The tip of her tongue stabbed his, as if reminding him she had desire, too.

The sheer, erotic force of their need made him groan. Ending their kiss, he suggested in a low growl, "Let's go back to your place."

"To make supper?"

There was amusement in his voice. "Do you

think we need to feed our bodies before we feed our lust?"

Now she became serious. "Is that what this is, Peter? Lust?"

"More than lust," he admitted huskily. But that was all he'd say. That was all he could say. If she was going to leave, that was all there was to say.

Although his body was still thrumming from the kiss and anticipation of what was to come, he didn't hurry the ride back and neither did she. It was as if they wanted to savor every moment, every nuance of whatever they shared— the shadows, the gleam of heavenly light, their horses' rocking motion as they walked the last half mile of their ride. A short time later they groomed Stormy and Dixie with deliberate care, their gazes connecting and holding, their desire for each other as thick as the scent of hay in the barn.

When they'd finished, they walked to the pool house, and now the cool night air carried a reality about it that Peter didn't want to face. Inside the pool house they washed up, Violet in the bathroom, him at the kitchen sink.

After she returned to the kitchen area she asked, "Pancakes, an omelet or both?"

He laughed. "Come to think of it, I haven't eaten since breakfast. Both sound good."

They worked side by side. He watched the eggs while she mixed the pancake batter. She took over the omelet while he poured and flipped pancakes on the griddle. They were so comfortable with each other, Peter felt as if he'd known Violet forever. He hadn't, and there was something he needed to talk to her about, something that had been gnawing at him since he'd seen her with Celeste this evening.

He waited until they were seated face-to-face at the table in the sitting area and had almost finished everything on their plates. "Celeste is getting attached to you."

"I'm getting attached to her," Violet responded with a smile.

"The truth is, I didn't think enough about that before I asked you to keep her company."

Violet laid down her fork. "Think enough about what?"

"She's lost too many people in her short life. When you leave, she'll lose you, too."

Silence was heavy around them until Violet asked, "Are you saying I should stop seeing her?"

Leaning back in his chair, he blew out a breath. "No, that's not what I'm saying. She needs your support. I just want you to keep in mind she sees you as more than a nurse or therapist."

"She sees me as a friend."

Not responding to that, Peter stood, picked up her plate as well as his, and took them over to the sink. Violet followed and ran water over the dishes, then added a dab of soap. As it bubbled, she peered down into the sink, and Peter knew he'd given her something to think about.

As he turned her to him, he said, "You're a compassionate woman who cares deeply. Just remember Celeste's feelings are running deep, too, because she's particularly vulnerable right now."

When Violet's blue eyes rose to his, he saw how vulnerable she was, too. He realized the nerve-thrumming desire that still rushed through him carried far too many questions that didn't have any answers. The unanswered questions carried so many complications they might not be able to unravel.

Serious now, he took her face between his palms. "Tell me something, Violet. Do you have affairs often?"

She didn't run from the question, and he read something sad and regretful in her eyes. "No, I don't," she confessed, as if she wished she didn't have to. "I haven't been with a man for years."

What had he been hoping she'd say? That she dated and slept with a different man every few weeks? Of course not. He'd known what her answer would be because of the vulnerability and innocence he sensed in her. No matter what he'd thought earlier, living in the moment with Violet Fortune would simply never be enough. That was why they had to put all of this into words.

"I'm not looking for one night. Or two or three. I'm searching for a lasting relationship and a commitment like my parents had. They looked in the same direction, had common values and agreed on how they were going to live their lives."

"My parents have that, too," she admitted quietly.

"Is there any chance you're going to be staying in Red Rock?" He braced himself for the answer he had to hear.

After a short hesitation, she shook her head. "No. My practice and my parents are in New York. I love the city."

"So Red Rock's still simply a getaway and a diversion?"

ggg222222

Although she hesitated a moment, she finally answered, "Yes."

Sliding his hands from her face, he knew what he had to do. He had to walk away. Today had been about exploration. His discoveries had confirmed how deeply he could become involved with Violet Fortune. But they could never have a relationship with her in New York and him in Red Rock—not one that would survive and thrive and rise above lust.

Knowing he was being abrupt, he didn't see another way to handle leaving. "I'd better get going. I have early surgery tomorrow."

"Chemistry's not enough, is it?" she asked, mirroring his thoughts.

"It's great for a night of distraction or a weekend fling. But I don't think either of us is looking for just that."

"We're all-or-nothing kind of people," she agreed.

Then he took her in his arms and he just held her. Finally, she pulled away and he let go. "I'll let you know when we transfer Celeste to Tumbleweed," he assured her.

"I'll be in to see her every day. You can leave a note for me at the nurses' desk."

"I'll call you." He wasn't going to avoid her. Yet there didn't seem to be anything more to say. If he stayed, his resolve to walk away might be as substantial as that mist on the lake.

At the door, he said, "Take care."

After she nodded, he left.

All the way home his body told him he was crazy for leaving. All the way home his mind told him he'd been practical and reasonable, and that was what had mattered. But all the way home he remembered Violet's face as they'd stood in the moonlight, and he swore, not at all sure he'd made the right decision.

Rodeos were an integral part of the Texas lifestyle. Violet sat in the stands next to Miles on Saturday night, her gaze on the ring. Quickly, she glanced over at Jessica and Clyde. They were holding hands and gazing at each other.

Violet smiled as the announcer's voice went over the next rider's statistics. She was watching steer wrestling, which wasn't one of her favorite events. If the rider's boot caught in the stirrup…

Adrenaline seemed to rush through the bleachers as the cowboy shot out of the chute. No sooner had he erupted from behind the wooden gate, he was propelling himself at the steer. His left hand reached for one horn, his right arm went around the other horn and his left leg kicked loose of the stirrup. Then he was on the ground trying to stop the steer. His horse, obviously expertly trained, veered off to the left, leaving the cowboy to wrestle the steer down.

Engrossed in the event and the raucous cheers of the audience all around her, Violet barely heard Stacey Clark say, "Imagine seeing you here."

Her attention drawn to Stacey's voice, she also saw Linda and then… Peter. There was shifting on the bench. Miles stood to greet the women and Peter, and he shook Peter's hand. Before Violet knew what had happened, Linda and Stacey had somehow managed to position Peter beside her.

After he lowered himself onto the bench, he glanced at her. "Didn't mean to intrude," he grumbled, as if this wasn't his idea at all. "Stacey saw your family sitting up here and decided it would be rude not to join you."

But Peter wouldn't have considered it rude not to join them, Violet was sure of that. He'd called her Thursday night to tell her Celeste was being moved to rehab on Friday. Violet had met him there to help the little girl settle in. He'd been cautiously friendly and absurdly polite, as if the wrong word or sentence would put them back into each other's arms. She supposed it could.

He'd left Tumbleweed yesterday before she had. As she'd spent the evening with Celeste last night, helping to acclimate her, an idea had come into her head that at first she'd considered ludicrous. But then it had taken shape and form, and the more she'd considered it the more it had appealed to her. She didn't know what Peter would think about it.

When she felt a prickling on her neck, she turned to see both Miles and Clyde watching her. Jessica just had a knowing smile on her face. As Violet looked in the opposite direction, she saw Stacey and Linda glancing at her and Peter. If they were trying their hand at match-making, it wasn't going to work.

Did she want it to work?

As if Peter had also become aware of curious stares from relatives, he frowned. "Did you eat supper?"

Violet shook her head.

"Let's go get a corn dog."

There were concession stands near the entrance to the rodeo, and Peter nodded in that direction.

In a denim shirt, jeans and boots tonight,

Peter looked more like a cowboy than a doctor. If she didn't know he was a doctor, she never would have guessed. He had so many facets, she knew she could spend a lifetime discovering them all.

A lifetime. What kind of dream was she weaving? If she wasn't careful, the threads of it would break apart in her fingers.

The night air was cooling, and she was glad she'd worn the navy flannel jacket. As they climbed down the bleachers and headed for the concession stands, the aromas of French fries, corn dogs and hamburgers rode on every breeze. Several men and women jostled past them, and the loudspeaker blared with the next event. Somehow, in the midst of all that, Violet was completely aware Peter was beside her, acutely sensitive to the brush of his elbow against hers, to the color of his eyes whenever he glanced her way.

"Celeste told me you stayed with her a long time last night," he remarked, leaning close to her ear so she could hear him.

When she looked up at him, caught by the mesmerizing sparks in his eyes, she just nodded. Then she realized he must have stopped in, too. "Did you see her today?"

"This afternoon after I made rounds. She's making friends and seems to be doing okay."

"When her therapy starts in earnest on Monday, I want to be there. Do you think that's all right?"

"Tumbleweed has an open-door policy for family. As her doctor, I can make sure you qualify."

There was an opening there if Violet wanted to take it. But there were too many people, too much noise, too much activity right now.

Instead of a corn dog, Violet ended up with a burger and a soda, as did Peter.

"Let's go this way," he directed her, and they headed for an area in back of the livestock that was fairly well-lit and quiet.

As they sat on stacked hay bales and ate, horses neighed, men shouted commands to each other inside and the loudspeaker seemed cranked up even higher. In spite of the commotion, Violet knew she had to take this opportunity to talk to Peter.

After she'd finished her burger, set the plate aside and sipped her soda, she blurted out, "I'm thinking about adopting Celeste."

Her nerve endings were already vibrating, just from being near Peter, and now his silence added to the sensation. "Say something," she murmured.

"I imagine you've given this a lot of thought."

"It's not a done deal. I'm still thinking about it. There's a lot to consider."

"Your career being the largest part of that."

"Yes, it is."

Finished with his burger, he turned the soda cup in his hand. "Even when Celeste is finished with rehab, she's going to need care and attention. She's been through a lot."

"And you don't think I can give her that care and attention?"

Setting the soda on the ground, his eyes locked to hers. "I think you can, if you concentrate on *her*. I don't think you can work sixty hours a week and do it."

She sighed. "That's what I'm trying to sort out. I can't make this commitment to Celeste until I decide where I want my professional life to go. But I just wanted you to know I was thinking about it."

"Well, now I know."

She wanted more from Peter than that, but she wasn't exactly sure what. "Tell me what you think of the idea."

"Violet, I can't know your mind." He sounded almost angry.

"Maybe you can, but I don't think you want to. I think you've walled yourself off against anything happening between us because it doesn't fit into some perfect plan of yours. You're a good doctor and a good man. But I think you want everyone to live up to your expectations."

"Maybe I just know what I need to be happy," he decided curtly.

"Maybe. Or maybe you won't let anyone break through your walls and make you happy."

His jaw set, his shoulders squared and straight, he informed her, "I have good reasons for those walls, Violet. I was serious about a woman before. I was committed to her and we were engaged. But then she was offered a grant to study overseas and in the blink of an eye, overnight, everything changed. Sandra aborted our baby. She said she had feelings for me, but she was just offered the experience of a lifetime and she wasn't going to give it up."

Whew! So there it was—the reason why Peter was so cautious. She could only imagine how he felt—not only losing his fiancée, but more important, losing his child. She knew about that kind of devastation.

"I'm so sorry, Peter. Didn't she tell you she was pregnant?"

Avoiding her gaze, he shook his head. "Not until it was over."

"Your relationship couldn't survive after she ended the pregnancy?" Violet asked.

"Sandra's grant would have lasted for four years. Even if I could have forgiven what she'd done—and I'm not sure I ever could have—we would only have seen each other maybe twice a year if we were lucky. I wanted a wife and a family and a real home, not a fly-by-night tryst in a tent in a desert when we could both squeeze it in."

There was so much pain behind Peter's words. He was speaking of what happened so matter-of-factly, but Violet knew there was betrayal there—a betrayal of love, and dreams, and a future. No wonder he wasn't eager to take a chance.

Looking at her now, he cupped her chin in his palm. "Could you ever abort a child?"

Violet solemnly shook her head. "Not ever. Life is too precious—" Her words caught as she thought about her own pregnancy that had never stood a chance.

Peter's voice was gravelly as he said, "You make me crazy, Violet. I'll admit that. You make me want to throw caution to the wind and ride the wild wave. But when that wave crashes, it's no fun. I've been there before, if you haven't. It takes too long to repair the damage."

"I know," she said simply.

Suddenly, there was a shout, and Violet heard her name being called. Then she saw Peter's dad and Charlene with Linda.

Charlene approached Violet with a wide smile. "Linda told me you were here and I didn't want to miss you."

Apparently Linda had kept her eye on them and knew where they'd gone.

"We just…got a bite to eat," Violet responded lamely.

Violet had risen at the sight of Peter's parents, and now Charlene took her aside while Peter's dad discussed the upcoming calf roping event with his son and daughter.

"We didn't have much time to talk at the anniversary party."

"You had lots of guests and I didn't want to take time away from them."

"You were a guest, too. Most of them don't really care about the work I do."

"You sound like my mother," Violet said with a laugh.

"What's she involved in?"

"Everything from making sure women take

advantage of their right to vote to encouraging dropouts to get a high school diploma. She's told me not to discuss those things with ordinary people because their eyes glaze over."

"I think I'd like to meet your mother."

Violet could see that Charlene meant it. "I don't think she's ever worked on a home for unwed mothers, though. And to tell you the truth, that does interest me."

With a curious look, Charlene said, "Then we should talk about it." She slipped a card from her jeans pocket. "Here's the address. I'm going to be there tomorrow afternoon, looking over what still needs to be accomplished before we can open. If you'd like to take a tour, I'll be there after one."

Violet glanced at Peter, but she knew this had nothing to do with him. Besides, she was interested. Tomorrow she could spend time with Celeste in the morning and then stop at the San Antonio address. "All right. I'll meet you there about one-thirty."

A few minutes later they all returned to the stands. But this time Violet didn't sit next to Peter. He wasn't the only one who had decisions to make.

Chapter 9

The house was in one of San Antonio's older neighborhoods. It was a two-story cream stucco with a red barrel-tile roof. There were porches on two sides and a small wrought-iron balcony off of one of the upstairs bedrooms. Violet went to the more formal entrance with its six concrete steps. Instead of using the knocker on the large brown door, she pressed the bell.

A few minutes later, Charlene opened the door, looking happy to see her. "You're just in time," she said.

"For what?"

"I'm pushing furniture around upstairs. You can help me decide what looks best and what's the most practical. Come on in and I'll give you the grand tour."

First Charlene showed her around the downstairs, which was sparsely furnished—a sofa in the living room, a table and chairs in the kitchen. Echoes sounded in all the rooms as their heels tapped against the wood floor. There were large, double-hung windows that looked brand-new, bare trim that needed a coat of paint and the smell of newly finished floors.

"It's a lovely house," Violet said as they walked from living room to dining room and through the kitchen. There were two rooms behind the kitchen and Violet asked, "What are you going to do with these?"

"One will be an office of sorts where the housemother can keep records, do paperwork, that kind of thing. The larger of the two will be her bedroom."

"You've found someone for the position?"

"Oh, yes. And she's perfect. Mrs. Mendoza is in her mid-fifties and has lots of energy. A widow with her children grown and scattered, she misses having somebody to take care of. In addition to Mrs. Mendoza, there will be an obstetrical nurse on call who will visit once a week, and a woman to help with the heavier cleaning and laundry. We'll expect the girls to take part in all the chores and the cooking, too." Charlene looked around, pride obvious in her eyes. "All the renovation work was done by volunteers and they did a wonderful job."

"They certainly did," Violet agreed. "When do you plan to open?"

"I'd like to start taking in girls after Thanksgiving. The trim needs to be painted, and I'm going to start working on that myself, tomorrow. Then I can move in more furniture I've been keeping in storage. It was all donated."

Violet glanced at the trim around the doors and the windows, the baseboard that was set in place but unfastened because it was waiting for stain or paint. "There's a lot of trim. Are you going to have help?"

"Unfortunately, no. My volunteers can only work weekends and I want to get this done." She gave Violet a sly smile. "If you have spare time on your hands…"

"I might," Violet responded with a laugh.

After Charlene showed Violet the upstairs, she said, "We're naming the house Haven. That's what I'd like it to be. A place where these girls can come and feel safe and wanted."

Never a willing traveler to go back in time and face teenage memories, Violet neverthe-less did it now. At fifteen, when she'd skipped one period and then two, she remembered how scared, unsure and entirely alone she'd felt.

"I have a coffeemaker in the kitchen. Would you like a cup?" Charlene asked.

"That sounds good."

From the moment she'd met Charlene, Violet had felt comfortable with her. After they'd fixed their coffee, they sat in the sunny living room on the sofa.

"So how did you get involved in all this?" Violet asked, curious about this woman Peter hadn't been able to warm up to.

After a very long pause, Charlene took another sip of her coffee and set the mug on the floor. "When I was sixteen, I got pregnant."

"What did you do?" Violet asked, wondering if Peter knew about this.

"I really didn't have a choice. I gave up my baby for adoption. My father had walked out when I was a kid and my mother said she wouldn't and couldn't raise another child." Charlene shrugged. "At sixteen, I didn't know where to go for help. My mother was as clueless as I was. When my family doctor suggested adoption, that's what I did."

"Did you have any time with your baby?" Violet asked wistfully.

"Only a few minutes after she was born.

They wouldn't even let me name her. They said her new parents would do that."

Charlene was about fifty-five, five years younger than Peter's dad. That meant her daughter would be about thirty-nine right now.

"I guess it was a closed adoption?"

"Sure was. In the early seventies there were still a lot of secrets. Many agencies and practitioners still believed a baby's life should be a clean slate, beginning with the adoption. Unfortunately, my mother chose one of those agencies."

"Then I guess you don't know where your daughter is."

Suddenly Charlene's face was alight with pleasure. "*Now* I do. I'd tried searching for her but couldn't get anywhere. The adoption agency we had used had closed its doors in the eighties and the records were lost. There wasn't a database for a P.I. to hack into. But I never gave up hope. About two years ago, George was on the Internet after buying a computer. He found one of those sites where a mother looking for an adopted child could register, or the child could register looking for biological parents. I signed up. A year went by without anything happening. But I was determined. I registered on a couple more similar sites. Then finally, last spring, I got an e-mail from one of the sites. My daughter wanted to meet me."

"Oh, my goodness! You must have been out of your mind with the joy of it."

"I was. But I was scared, too, not knowing how she would react or if we'd ever have a relationship past the reunion."

"But you had a reunion?"

"Yes, we did. She lives in California, so George and I took a vacation out there in March. She has a wonderful family, a great husband and two kids. We're getting to know each other slowly, mostly through e-mails. I'm hoping maybe she and her family will come join us this Christmas."

"Peter never mentioned any of this."

"That's because he doesn't know. Neither do Stacey and Linda."

"Why?"

Charlene's hands fluttered nervously. "Even though it was a long time ago, settling into the Clark family wasn't easy. George was wonderful. He never made me feel like a second wife, or less than Estelle, or as if I were in competition with her. But the kids... At first Linda and Stacey kept their distance, but slowly they let me love them. I have a great relationship with them now—a real friendship. But Peter...

He saw all the differences between me and his mother. I was younger, I had a job, and with two incomes George and I could do things he and Estelle hadn't. I convinced him to learn how to water-ski. I know it sounds like a small thing, but Peter looked at his dad and thought he'd forgotten all about his mother."

"His dad married you about a year after Estelle died."

"Yes, and looking back now, I see we should have waited. I think, deep down, Peter believed I knew his father before his mom died. But that wasn't true. George and I met at a builders' show, of all places. I was manning a stand for my boss, who sold bathtubs and showers and that kind of thing. George had simply been trying to wile away a lonely afternoon. We connected on the spot, for whatever reason. On the first few dates he talked mostly about Estelle, but then we quickly moved beyond that." Charlene looked away for a moment, as if reminiscing, then said, "Well, at least Peter tolerates me now."

Violet smiled. "I think it's more than that. Maybe he doesn't want to admit it, but I think he admires and respects you. When are you going to tell him about— What's your daughter's name?"

"Her name's Taylor, and I was thinking I'd tell him after Thanksgiving."

"I don't think you have to worry about Stacey and Linda. My guess is they'll welcome Taylor into the family." When Violet thought about what had happened to her at fifteen, she pictured how everything would have been different if her pregnancy had been a normal one.

"Why so sad?" Charlene asked.

Violet hadn't suspected her emotions were showing. "Your home for unwed mothers interests me because I was almost one of them."

"Go on," Charlene encouraged.

"I don't know if you know anything about the Fortunes, but I came from a privileged background."

"There are always stories and rumors, just like the rumors now about how Ryan Fortune is really connected to Christopher Jamison, and why Jamison had the crown birthmark."

"That's Ryan's story to tell," Violet said quietly. The whole background of Ryan and Kingston Fortune hadn't been made public yet. Although she trusted Charlene could keep a confidence, she wasn't going to break the family's silence.

"Of course it's his story to tell. That's the whole point," Charlene agreed. "People might speculate about the Fortunes, but they don't really know them. Isn't that what you're saying?"

"Exactly. I guess when I was a child growing up, even my family didn't know me. I tagged along after my brothers, but they were older. My dad worked terribly long hours, my mom had her causes. I felt left out. So I went looking for the wrong kind of validation."

"A boy who wanted you."

"Yes. Then I didn't know the difference between sex and love. I thought if he wanted to have sex with me, that meant he loved me. Anyway, I got pregnant at fifteen. But I didn't tell anyone. I wanted that baby—someone of my very own to love. I thought if I let the pregnancy go long enough, no one could do anything about it. What I didn't know was that it was an ectopic pregnancy. I was keeping to myself a lot, scared about the whole thing. One weekend I was in my room doing schoolwork, and I had sharp pains. They were so bad I ended up on the floor. My mother must have had a sixth sense or something because she came in and found me. They rushed me to the hospital and had to do surgery. I almost died."

"Oh, Violet. I'm so sorry."

Even now, talking about it, Violet could feel the tightness in her chest, the loss she still felt of a pregnancy gone awry. Swallowing hard, she said, "It was a long time ago."

"Giving away Taylor for adoption was a long time ago, too. But some things always stay vivid in our minds."

There was a bond forming between her and Charlene based on understanding each other's experiences.

"Have you told Peter all of this?" Charlene asked.

"No. Peter and I— Neither of us seems to be gamblers when it comes to relationships. There are so many obstacles between us that we're both playing it very safe."

"If I would have played it safe, I never would have married Peter's father. Talk about obstacles—a mother who was considered almost an angel, children to win over, a household to run when I'd only lived by myself before. But if I hadn't taken the risk, I'd have missed so much. You can't think of it as gambling and winning or losing. You have to think of it as stepping out in faith, reaching for more than you have now, reaching for *someone*."

The way Charlene said it, Violet knew she meant every word. "I'll think about what you said."

"Good. Because Peter needs someone to

reach out to him. He needs someone to shake up the world he's built for himself. Surely there can be a lot more to it. In the meantime, I could use some help with painting this trim. How are you with a paintbrush?"

"I haven't painted anything lately," Violet said with a little laugh. "But I'm game."

"What's better for you, morning or afternoon?"

"I can spend some time with Celeste in the morning, then come in for the afternoon. Does that work?"

"That works just fine. Make sure you bring old clothes."

The following afternoon, Violet raised her brush to paint the door trim, and off-white paint dripped onto her jeans. She rolled her eyes, putting her brush to the door frame again, and listened to the oldies music on Charlene's radio.

When the front door of the house opened, Violet didn't even turn around as she took the paintbrush the whole way down to the floor, covering the remainder of the trim. During the few hours she'd been helping Charlene, an electrician and a plumber had come and gone, as well as the workman who had finished paneling one of the upstairs rooms.

Charlene's "This is a surprise!" didn't even distract Violet as she concentrated on keeping the edge of her brush straight.

"I'm looking for Violet. Her voice mail picked up on her cell. When I called the Flying Aces, Clyde told me she'd be here."

The sound of Peter's voice stopped Violet's hand midstroke. She'd left her cell phone in the car. This morning, when she'd had breakfast with her brothers and Jessica, she'd told them what she'd be doing today. Maybe that had been fortunate, and maybe it hadn't.

Slowly she turned, and her gaze met Peter's. "Celeste is all right, isn't she?" She'd spent time with her this morning and had lunch with her before she'd left.

"Celeste is fine."

Just then, Charlene's cell phone sounded from the pocket of the smock she wore over her clothes. "I'll be right back," she said and went into the kitchen.

Even though Charlene disappeared beyond the doorway, Peter still lowered his voice. "I wanted to tell you about Ryan. I've convinced him to take the spot in the clinical trials. We're flying to New York on Thursday. I've already called Houston and had all his paperwork sent up."

"I'm surprised you changed his mind. He sounded very definite about not wanting to do it."

"A couple of things played into this. The fact that your parents are in New York, and he could stay with them if he decides to start treatment. I explained about my mother and how any extra time with her would have benefitted us. He took it all into consideration. I can't say he's totally enthusiastic about the whole idea, but I think if we get him up there, let him talk to the doctor, learn about the program, he'll get back his fighting spirit. You'll probably be getting a call from him. He wants you to go along."

"Me?"

"He feels you're his doctor, too. And he's right about that. He came to you first. I think your moral support means a lot to him."

She chewed on her lower lip for a moment. "I guess we'll have to stay overnight. We can stay at my place. I wonder if Ryan will tell my parents about his condition this trip or wait until he's in the program."

"He wants to see if he's accepted into the program and what the treatment entails. Like I said, he's not one hundred percent sold. Apparently he has a friend in New York, and he's thinking about staying with him overnight."

"Do you think he'll confide in his friend?"

"I don't know."

"I want to call him, but I'm afraid he won't be able to talk. I guess I'll just have to wait until he calls me. Thanks for stopping to tell me." She suddenly realized she must look a mess. There were paint splatters on her jeans and on her blouse. She might even have some on her face from painting the top of the doorway.

Peter was looking at her lips as if a dab of paint might have found its way there.

When Charlene returned to the room, she was frowning. "I can't believe the bureaucracy when I'm just trying to help kids in need." Her cheeks were pink and she looked agitated.

"A problem?" Peter asked.

"Nothing that can't be solved, though we might not be able to open on time. I have to fill out more papers, get more approvals." She shook her head. "All I want to do is take care of these teenagers who have no place to go and no one to turn to."

"Why do you care so much about this?" Peter asked, looking as if he were truly interested in the answer.

After a very long look at Violet and a deep breath, Charlene turned to her stepson.

"Maybe I should leave," Violet murmured.

"No. Stay. You know what I'm going to say, and why this is important to me."

Peter's eyebrows arched, as if he wondered why Violet would know and he didn't.

"When I was sixteen," Charlene said in a low voice, "I was an unwed mother and gave up my baby for adoption."

To Peter's credit, if he was shocked by the news, he kept it well hidden. "What did you have?" he asked kindly. "A boy or a girl?"

"I had a girl. Last year we found each other through the Internet. I was going to tell you and your sisters about it soon."

"Stacey and Linda don't know?"

"No. No one knows but your father. And Violet. We were just talking and it came out."

"But in the past year, it didn't come out to Stacey or Linda or me?"

At that moment, Charlene looked incredibly vulnerable as she said, "I didn't know what you'd think about me after I told you."

"You were sixteen. I imagine you didn't have much of a choice."

Tears glistened in her eyes now. "No, I didn't."

Quickly checking her watch, Charlene removed her smock and folded it over her arm. "I'm going to go home for a bit, get something to eat with your dad, then try to convince him to come back here with me later." She looked at the doorway Violet had finished. "You did a great job. Just wash out your brush and put it in that bucket in the kitchen after you're through. When you leave, turn the lock on the door and close it. Give me a call sometime, and we'll have lunch together, okay?"

Violet could see that Charlene was embarrassed by what she'd told Peter, that she needed to leave to get her bearings. Now that she'd told *him,* she'd probably want to tell Stacey and Linda, too.

"Sure. I'll give you a call. This is going to be a great place, Charlene. You'll do a lot of good here."

With a small smile and a wave, Charlene picked up her purse in the kitchen and then left.

"I'm going to wash out my brush," Violet said and went into the kitchen.

There was an oak table with four plank-bottom chairs. Peter came in after her, pulled one out and sat down. He seemed to be lost in thought as she washed out her brush, then went back to the living room, covered her can of paint and set it aside.

Peter was still in the kitchen looking thoughtful when she'd finished. "I've never tried to get to know Charlene," he said without preamble. "No wonder she didn't tell me she had a child."

Hearing the regret in his voice, Violet pulled out a chair and sat beside him. "You can still get to know her."

"It might be too late to mend fences. All these years I think I felt, subconsciously, if I made a connection to her, I was being disloyal to my mother's memory."

"You felt you had to preserve it because your dad didn't."

His gaze was sad when it met hers. "I suppose that's true."

"I don't think it's ever too late to mend fences, especially if that's what you both want. And I don't think Charlene has held any grudges."

"That in itself is amazing."

"You can't make someone love you if he or she doesn't want to love you. The only thing you can do is let go and wait."

His gaze fell on her and lingered. "How did you get so smart?"

"A long time ago I went looking for love and thought I'd found it. I hadn't. Now I think I can spot the genuine emotion."

"Long ago. Was that one man in particular?"

If she told Peter about her past, would he think less of her? Or would it tighten their bond? They *did* have one, whether they wanted it or not. "It was a boy, not a man," she confided quietly.

"What happened?" In his eyes there was a real need to know, and she realized she couldn't keep anything from him. "I told you I was lonely as a teenager."

"All that testosterone in the house," he suggested with a small smile.

"That was definitely part of it."

"And your parents were involved in their own lives."

"You know how it is when you're a teenager. You don't want to need them or depend on them, and you give them that impression. Yet, deep down, you really do."

When he nodded, she realized he did know. After all, he'd lost a parent, and the other one had moved on before Peter was ready. "I was only fifteen. But I thought I was old enough for anything I wanted to do. Then a football player asked me out. It developed into a lot more than a soda and a hamburger. A few weeks later when I missed a period, I knew how stupid I'd been." She watched Peter's expression for his reaction.

"Or been taken advantage of," he muttered.

His green eyes were piercingly intent as he waited for her story.

"It was my own fault. My mother had given me The Talk. I don't know if I was rebelling, or just wanted someone of my own so badly I didn't care. I still kept everything to myself. I thought if I hid my condition for long enough, no one could do anything about it. I don't know what I thought I was going to do with a baby, but I did want it. I was in my third month when I collapsed one weekend. My mother found me and rushed me to the hospital."

Taking a breath, she searched Peter's face. There was no judgment there—just compassion. "I had an ectopic pregnancy and it ruptured. After surgery I found out how much my mom and dad and my brothers really did love me. They helped me through it. My mom and I had long talks about important things. I decided I wanted to accelerate my education so I could get through high school quicker, and she found me a tutor." Violet smiled. "Then she came home with career counseling questionnaires and I made up my mind I wanted to be a doctor."

"I see why you can understand how much Charlene wants to help teenagers in crises."

With Peter sitting so close, Violet could smell

his cologne and see lines of fatigue around his eyes. She could feel his curiosity about her life, and what she'd become. She could also feel the hum of sexual tension that always seemed to surround them and made her nerve endings tingle.

After a long pause, Peter asked, "What would you have done if you'd have gotten pregnant in med school?"

During the time she'd known Peter, she realized he didn't ask idle questions. "I would have kept the baby. I could never give up a child." There were shadows in Peter's eyes that came from doubts. "Do you believe me?"

Leaning away from her, as if their magnetic pull toward each other was too potent and he'd kiss her if he didn't, he frowned. "You're a Fortune. You could have hired a nanny. You could have gone on with your life either way."

"I *never* would have hired a nanny. My brothers and I had a nanny until I was about ten, and I hated it."

"You said you were thinking about adopting Celeste. If you do that, would you hire someone to take care of her?"

Peter was fishing, giving her some type of pop quiz, and she didn't know if she was passing the test. Resenting his questions now, she answered, "I'm not sure. I would probably hire a housekeeper to help."

"Celeste will need one-on-one care for a while. A housekeeper won't be a solution to that."

"I don't have all the answers yet, Peter."

"You're going to have to have answers before you make a decision about Celeste."

Suddenly he stood, took her hand and tugged her up. "Do you have plans for tonight?"

"No," she responded flatly, bothered by his questions.

"Then come home with me. I want to show you something."

Come home with me.

She liked the sound of that. She liked the *idea* of it even more. If she went home with Peter tonight...

She'd handle one emotion at a time and hope her heart was leading her in the right direction.

Chapter 10

After Violet followed Peter home in her car, he put on a pot of coffee and motioned her to the sofa in the great room. She was curious about what he wanted to show her. More than that, she admitted to herself, she loved being with him.

Loved being with him?

All right. She was falling in love with him.

Crossing to the cupboard in the entertainment center, he crouched down and pulled out two photo albums. When he returned to where Violet was sitting, he lowered himself beside her and placed them on her lap. "Take a look at these," he said, his face very serious.

As soon as she began paging through them, she recognized Peter and his two sisters. In the first ones, he looked to be about five, Linda and Stacey merely toddlers. With them, she noticed the same kind-expressioned woman whom she'd seen in the pictures in his curio cabinet the first night she'd been here with Ryan. His father must have been taking the pictures because he was only in a few of them. As she watched Peter and Stacey and Linda grow before her eyes, she remembered her own childhood with her brothers.

After Peter turned around eight, there were other children in the photos on and off. Although the core family stayed the same, other kids came and went. There were at least six different ones.

"Are these the foster children your mother and dad took in?"

"Some of them." He pointed to each one and named them. "They live all over the U.S. and the world now. My mom cared for each one of them as if they were her own, no matter how long they stayed with us. Some were here a month, some over a year. She never worked outside the home, but her work was so important. These kids could have ended up on the streets or in abusive situations. No matter how tight money was, somehow she always stretched it."

Violet heard the subtle message he was giving her—he wanted to marry a woman whose only concern was her family. She didn't feel he was being chauvinistic about it, simply that that was what was right for him. But she didn't know if he was being realistic.

"Taking care of children is important, but work and careers matter, too, Peter. If a woman is talented and educated in some area, should she give that up to have a family?"

Raking his hand through his hair, he studied her for a long time. "I don't know. I just know the kind of hours I work and the amount of love and care and attention children need. Even if I never get married, when I retire, I want to take in foster kids."

His green eyes seemed to be asking her a deep, important question.

"That's a wonderful idea. So many kids need a good home. Because of the surgery I had with the ectopic pregnancy, I could have trouble conceiving." As she watched his expression she went on, "I guess that's another reason I'm considering adopting Celeste and why when I'm ready to have a family, I would consider adopting more kids."

"Having children of my own isn't a big deal," he admitted in a husky tone.

Violet hadn't realized she was holding her breath, waiting for his response. Now, as his hands slid under her hair and his thumb caressed her cheek, she felt as if she could melt right there on the sofa. So much was right between her and Peter. Yet she wasn't sure she was the type of woman he wanted or needed.

"I can't seem to stay away from you." He didn't sound at all happy about that.

Suddenly, everything about Peter tempted her unbearably. After they'd come in, he'd removed his suit coat and tie and unbuttoned the top two buttons of his shirt. She could see a whorl of chest hair, and her fingers tingled to feel his skin under it.

"When you look at me like that, Violet, you're asking to be kissed."

"When you look at me like that," she returned, "I want you to kiss me."

His low groan when he covered her mouth with his told her he'd lost his battle of resisting the chemistry between them. The hunger in his kiss told her he was embracing it wholeheartedly. Yet as his tongue teased her lips open, as he pushed inside and took her, she knew this encounter was about a lot more than chemis-

Karen Rose Smith 211

try and attraction. Neither of them wanted a shallow fling. She guessed neither of them was *capable* of a shallow fling. Everything about Peter's desire for her and her response to it was serious. However, the seriousness didn't erase questions and elusive answers.

Along with the intimate motion of Peter's tongue, he touched her...touched her in ways she'd never been touched before. Not intimately at first, but infinitely tender. While his tongue awakened every erotic desire she could imagine, his hands stroked her hair. After a few exquisite seconds, Peter's large hands slid to her shoulders, then to the buttons on her blouse. When he began unfastening them, she found herself pulling his shirt from his trousers.

Tearing his mouth from hers, he stared into her eyes. "I want you, Violet. I want you more than I ever thought possible."

She wanted him, too. Permanently. Absolutely. Irrevocably. Her mouth was dry, her throat clogged, and she couldn't seem to find any words. Passion had never taken hold of her this forcefully and overwhelmingly before. In fact, she realized now, she'd never known true passion before. Not like this.

Reaching for the placket of his shirt, she unbuttoned the buttons quickly. He finished hers.

As she shrugged out of her blouse, he shrugged out of his shirt. They couldn't take their eyes from each other.

With excruciating slowness, he traced the cup of her bra and she shivered. "I've imagined you naked," he said in a ragged voice.

Reaching out, she flattened her palms on his chest, then ran her thumbs over his nipples. "I've touched you naked in my dreams."

Then she slid her hand down the middle of his chest, and he closed his eyes. Boldly she reached for his belt buckle and unfastened it.

But when her hand went to his fly, he covered it with his. "You'd better let me do that."

"Why?"

"Because I want to give you pleasure before I'm beyond my limits."

The idea of Peter beyond his limits excited her and aroused her even more fully. As his arms went around her to unfasten her bra, he kissed her cheek and teased her ear with his lips.

"Peter," she moaned.

"What?" Her bra unfastened now, he slipped the straps from her shoulders and cupped her breasts in his palms.

"You're making me...crazy," she said on a ragged breath.

"You've been doing that to me since the first

moment I met you. Let's get the rest of your clothes off."

He did that and shucked his, too. Then they were in each other's arms again.

Peter's scent was pure male. His muscles were so taut and well-defined, his desire for her hot and heavy and enveloping. Within moments he had her lying on her back on the sofa. He fished in his pants pockets for his wallet, prepared himself with a condom and stretched on top of her. But he didn't hurry to join them. He was prolonging their pleasure until they were *both* at their limit.

As he kissed her breasts, his tongue laving her nipples, she could feel the connection in her womb. Her skin glistened as he kissed lower, and she became more restless, knowing she needed more, not wanting his kisses to end, but searching for the fulfillment only he could provide.

"Peter, I'm ready."

"I'm going to make sure," came his deep growl.

Moving still lower, his tongue teased her stomach, and her hands laced in his short, thick hair. She wanted him in her arms. She wanted to feel his body tight against hers. But she couldn't stop him now. He was giving her so much pleasure she almost couldn't stand it.

When he reached her navel, his tongue flicked around it until she murmured his name. He looked up at her and grinned at her, asking, "More?"

"I don't know if I can handle much more," she answered shakily.

"Oh, I think you can handle a lot more."

The promise in his voice scared her. What if she didn't respond to him? What if nothing he did brought her to climax? "Peter, it doesn't matter. I mean, if nothing happens, it's not your fault. I'm just not very responsive."

"Hogwash."

"Hogwash?" She almost smiled at him.

"I would have used something stronger but it didn't seem appropriate right now. You're a passionate woman, Violet. Your kisses have been the closest thing I've ever felt to a cyclone hitting me. So I'm not going to believe that you have a problem responding."

"I just wanted you to know—"

"Oh, I know. I know you're going to enjoy this." Then his tongue and his lips went lower still.

When he caressed her thighs, she felt wild and wanton. As he kissed above the nest of her hair, then with infinite slowness separated the petals of her womanhood and kissed there, too, she could hardly catch her breath. She could hardly remember her name.

And she'd been afraid she wouldn't respond to him?

Peter's mouth was hot and wet. In a few moments she was reaching for his shoulders, gasping in pleasure, amazed by the wondrously erotic sensations coursing through her. So this was an orgasm. This was what rocketing to the moon felt like. This was what loving a man and accepting pleasure from him was all about.

He didn't give her time to savor the tingles. He didn't give her time to think about what came next. Instead, he rose above her, propping a forearm on either side of her, his body long and lean and glistening.

"Lift your knees," he suggested.

As she did, he entered her. It was a long, smooth thrust that had her wrapping her legs around him. They were joined in the most intimate way a man and woman could be joined. She felt the lingering tingles building into another explosion as he slowly withdrew then drove into her again, faster and deeper. He knew exactly what he was doing because each time he withdrew, each time he united with her again, he pushed her higher and higher into erotic sensation that made stars dance in front of her eyes.

Her nails dug into his shoulders. "Peter, it's so wonderful."

"Yes, it is," he agreed, and then kissed her—a full, openmouthed kiss that was greedy and masterful and thoroughly intoxicating.

She held on to him as he took her on a journey with him—a journey through a dark universe. As he shifted, she cried out because the pleasure was so erotic. Then she called his name again as an incredible climax began to build, stronger, higher, more encompassing than the first. It swept over her and shook her until a thousand stars burst in front of her eyes. Poised on the edge of the sublime, then toppling over that edge, she called Peter's name. His body went taut, and she felt his control finally crumble as he thrust into her and shuddered over and over again.

He lay on top of her until they were both breathing more normally, then he shifted his legs to the floor and sat on the edge of the sofa, catching his breath. She sat up, suddenly realizing exactly what they'd done.

Turning toward her, his hand covering hers, he intertwined their fingers.

Before either of them could speak, a Samba

melody came from Violet's purse that was sitting on the coffee table—her cell phone.

"I'd better get that. It could be Ryan or my parents."

Peter didn't argue the point, and she wondered if he was glad for some time to think about what had just happened. He motioned to the bathroom and disappeared down the hall.

When she opened her phone and answered with a shaky hello, Miles asked, "Where are you?"

"It's nice to hear from you, too, bro."

She heard Miles's weary sigh. "We were worried. We've been waiting for you to come back."

"We?"

"Jessica, Clyde and me. We need to discuss something with you."

"What? It can't wait till morning?"

"You won't be back until morning?"

Glancing down the hall, she responded, "I didn't say that." She didn't know how Peter was feeling right now, exactly what making love had meant to him. "What did you want to talk to me about?"

"A barbecue. Clyde and Jessica want to give one and invite everybody they care about. They got the idea when Dad called. He and Mom are flying in tomorrow for a visit before they go on vacation in New Orleans."

"How long are they staying?"

"Just two or three days. Dad wants to talk to Ryan and I think Mom just wants to welcome Jessica into the family again. So we're making plans for a barbecue tomorrow night. Will you be free?"

"I'll make sure I'm free. We can talk about it at breakfast."

"At 6:00 a.m.?" Miles was an early riser.

Violet groaned. "I'll be there. Does it have to be six?"

He chuckled. "It has to be six. It's the only way I can get everything in I have to do. Ranches don't run themselves." His voice turned sober again. "So you'll be home soon?"

Peter had returned to the room and now pulled on his trousers.

"Yes, soon. Go to bed, Miles. I don't need a keeper."

After a grunt from her brother, and an "I'll see you at breakfast," he hung up.

Now, feeling self-conscious about her nakedness, Violet closed her phone and dropped it once more into her purse.

"The brother brigade looking for you?" Peter asked, still shirtless and abominably sexy.

"You could say that. Sometimes I feel as if

they want me to give them an itinerary before I go anywhere, do anything or see anyone."

"They probably do."

Quickly she slipped into her bra and fastened it, then added her blouse. The silence between her and Peter filled the room.

"You're thinking about what that meant, aren't you?" Peter asked as she drew up her panties and stepped into her jeans.

"Aren't you?"

"It's probably better if we don't dissect it."

"Maybe if we dissect it, we won't repeat it."

Taking her by the shoulders, Peter studied her for a few long moments, then slid his hands into her hair, brought her face close to his and murmured, "Once wasn't nearly enough."

His kiss was hard and demanding, and she felt his turmoil as much as her own. What had they done? What had they started? Where were they going to go from here?

"Don't even try to answer the questions tonight," he ordered. "Maybe we'll get some answers if we just play this by ear."

Again there was that silence of a thousand words unsaid. Breaking the quiet, she murmured, "I'd better go." Testing the waters, testing where they were headed, she added, "Clyde and Jessica are having a barbecue tomorrow night. My parents are flying in. Would you like to come?"

When he didn't answer right away, she hurried to say, "You don't have to tell me now. In fact, you don't have to tell me at all. If you find yourself free and you want to come to the ranch—"

"It might be late, but I'll be there, unless I get tied up in an emergency. If that happens, I'll call you."

When she picked up her purse, he walked her to the door.

She was at a complete loss for words, and it seemed he was too. As she put her hand on the doorknob to leave, she wished he'd stop her. She wished he'd ask her to stay the night. But there was still too much uncertainty about what they both wanted.

He didn't ask her to stay.

So she left Peter Clark's house, her body still thrumming from the way he'd made love to her. Their intimacy had made her feel even more vulnerable. Now that she'd given her body to him, she'd also given her heart.

As she slipped into her car and switched on the ignition, she was more afraid than she'd ever been in her life. She might not be the kind of woman he wanted. If that was true, he might hand her heart right back.

Pulling away from the curb in front of Peter's house, she thought again of Celeste and the decisions she had to make.

When would she be sure she was be making the right ones?

Peter couldn't wait to see Violet.

The feeling was so foreign to him that he wasn't sure quite what to do with it.

When he arrived at the Flying Aces, the barbecue was in full swing. Miles welcomed him. Clyde looked him over a few more times. Jessica pointed out her sister, Leslie, and her husband, Marty, who owned a hardware store in town. Then she made the rounds with him, introducing him to Patrick Fortune, Violet's dad, who was sitting at a table with Ryan and Lily, and Savannah and Cruz Perez. Savannah was nine months pregnant and Cruz was positioning a small hay bale for her to prop her feet on.

Jessica explained, "Savannah has to take it easy for the rest of her pregnancy, but she needed to get out and see friends. Cruz isn't letting her move a muscle."

As she looked over the gathered guests, Jessica finally admitted, "I don't know where Violet is. She was here just a little while ago. Her mother's disappeared, too."

Just then, a couple came from around the side of the house. When they approached Jessica, Steven and Amy Fortune, Violet's brother and his wife, said their hellos.

"We're surrounded by Fortunes," Jessica said amiably, as Steven and Peter shook hands.

"You're one now, too," Amy kidded. "Just like I am."

"I guess I am," Jessica responded with a smile. "Everything happened so fast with me and Clyde it still doesn't seem real. Have you seen Violet?"

Steven nodded. "She and Mom were going into the barn. She probably just wants to introduce Mom to the new horse."

"I can find my way," Peter told Jessica. "Stay with your guests."

"Tell Violet we're serving desserts in fifteen minutes. That should get her back here. If you don't know it yet, she has a sweet tooth."

Peter already suspected sweets tempted Violet from her comments at the restaurant when they'd gone to the Riverwalk. She'd sensually savored every bite of that white chocolate cheesecake. It had driven him crazy.

Before he'd left the hospital, he'd changed

into jeans and a western-cut shirt. Now he was glad he had. He'd guessed the barbecue would be casual, and it was.

Familiar with the barn that housed the horses from his night ride with Violet, Peter went to a side door and opened it. Dusk had been taken over by the deeper shadows of night, and the sky was murky with clouds that slid over the crescent moon. Tonight only a few stars were evident, unlike the night he and Violet had taken their ride.

Inside the barn, he headed for the glow of yellow light over the walkway between the stalls. His footsteps were muted by hay as he passed the tack room and heard women's voices.

Violet's was more than recognizable as she said, "I think I need more in my life than work. Maybe that's why I'm having such a tough time getting over Anne Washburn's death and her baby's. I don't have a balance."

Violet's mother responded, "You've always been so focused. I didn't think you wanted anything else."

"I didn't, either."

"You've worked so hard. You've earned such a good reputation. You can't be thinking about giving it all up!"

"Let me ask you something," Violet said

softly. "If you had to choose between making the world a better place, and marrying Dad and having a family, which would you choose?"

"You can't ask me a question like that."

"Sure, I can. Causes have been your career. What if you could only have one? The family or the work?"

"That's really not a fair question, Violet. I love you, your father and your brothers with all of my heart. But I'm also the type of woman who needs something else."

Peter knew Lacey Fortune's nonanswer was sending Violet a message.

He'd never meant to eavesdrop and he didn't want to continue doing it. When he approached the two women, Lacey was the first one to see him emerging from the shadows. Her eyebrows rose and she looked to Violet.

Violet's smile for him made him almost forget what he'd heard…almost made him put aside everything he considered an obstacle between them. He experienced a lightness in his heart, along with a racing pulse, as he smiled back.

"You made it!" She was obviously happy to see him.

"I told you I would." One thing Violet had to learn about him was that he never broke his word.

"Dr. Peter Clark, this is my mother, Lacey

Fortune. Mom, Peter is the neurosurgeon who operated on Celeste."

Lacey was in her late-sixties, about five foot ten with gray-blond hair and green eyes. Even in jeans she was as elegant and beautiful as her daughter.

Peter extended his hand to her and she shook it. "It's good to meet you."

"It's good to meet *you.*"

Maybe he should have listened in on that conversation a little longer. He wasn't sure what Violet might have revealed about him or their relationship.

"You're the bachelor Miles told me about." Lacey's eyes twinkled.

"I'll never live down that auction," he groaned with a shake of his head.

Lacey laughed, then added, "Well, I'm going to head back to the barbecue. Jessica said something about chocolate mousse cake. That sounds too good to turn down."

"It's almost dark. Would you like me to walk you back?" Peter offered.

"Oh, no. I can find my way. I always have, and I always will." There was a last, knowing glance at her daughter, then she went through the barn the way Peter had come.

Seconds later Peter heard the barn door close.

Night sounds in the barn—horses moving in their stalls, the creak of barnwood, a cat jumping atop a stall—danced between them until Violet broke the silence. "While we're alone, I wanted to tell you I had a few private moments with Ryan. He does want me to go to New York, and he's telling Lily that's where we're going. I'll take the opportunity to stop in at my office while we're there and catch up on anything I've missed. I don't need an excuse, and Ryan's relying on the cover of business again."

"She'll probably believe it if she knows you two are going together. I'll meet you at the airport."

Violet was standing in front of the stall and now he put one hand on either side of her. "While we're alone, I can think of better things to do than to talk about our flight."

"Such as?" Violet asked coyly.

"Such as this."

When his lips covered hers, memories of their union on his sofa came flooding back. Violet's perfume always enticed him. Her soft, silky hair in his hands was a sensual delight. And her mouth… Her lips were responsive to his, and her kiss was everything he'd hoped it would be. He'd missed her, and he didn't un-

derstand that, any more than he understood his
need for her. The smell of hay, the cool October
night, the swishing of horses's tails seemed to
belong in another dimension. They kissed as
if they'd never kissed before and might never
kiss again. As he leaned into her, their lower
bodies fit together perfectly, and he groaned
when she moved against him.

Could they get away with making love here
while the party was going on out there? He'd
never even considered doing anything so reckless before.

One of his hands went to the buttons on her
blouse and he began unfastening them. Her fingers went to his shirt and plucked it from his
jeans. Then her hand slid against his skin and
he sucked in a breath.

"This is insane," he muttered as she sifted
through his chest hair and he could hardly
breathe.

He trailed kisses down her neck and his hand
cupped her breast. Her moan of approval told
him the first vacant stall would have to afford
them all the privacy they were going to get.

Violet was getting bolder now and her hand
cupped him. They *might* make it to the stall.

Suddenly, the barn door flew open and Miles

yelled inside, "Violet! Peter! Savannah's water broke. We need you."

The same way Peter came instantly awake in the middle of the night when he was paged, now his hands dropped to his side and his gaze met Violet's.

She fought the haze of the passion they'd shared and called to her brother, "We'll be right there."

"Damn!" Peter muttered as he buttoned his shirt and tucked it into his jeans.

"I second that," she agreed, righting her clothes, too. Peter knew they had to talk about her conversation with her mother, about how foolish they were being, about what the future held in store for them. But they couldn't do that now.

"It's been a long time since med school and a rotation in obstetrics," he muttered.

When Violet didn't respond, he could see she'd gone back in time and was revisiting memories. "Is being with Savannah or any pregnant woman hard for you?"

"Not really. Not anymore. I just wonder what would have happened if my pregnancy hadn't been ectopic."

"Don't do that to yourself." He put his arm around her and brought her close, holding her

next to his chest. "Come on. Let's go make sure
Savannah has a safe delivery, no matter how
and where it happens."

With his arm around Violet, they walked
through the barn and out into the night.

Chapter 11

Violet, Peter and Cruz stood before the nursery's glass window.

Cruz was absolutely beaming. "Just look at her wave her hands. I can't believe she's my daughter."

"If you don't believe it," Violet said with a laugh, "just ask Savannah."

"She was a trouper," Peter agreed. "I was amazed at how calm she was during the trip to the hospital."

After Savannah's water had broken at the barbecue, labor pains had begun with vicious intensity. Cruz had insisted on driving his wife to the hospital, but Peter had volunteered to drive while Cruz attended to his wife. Savannah had asked Violet to come along, too.

Within an hour after they'd reached the hospital, little Rose had been born.

"She's got a healthy start on life. Eight pounds, four ounces isn't anything to sneeze at."

Violet wasn't just watching Cruz's expression, but Peter's, too.

"I'm going to call the family and tell them we have a beautiful baby daughter. Then I'm going to see how Savannah's doing," Cruz said. "She might be sleeping. I'm sure labor and delivery tired her out. Thanks for coming along with us. That helped a lot."

"Congratulations again," Peter said.

Violet gave Cruz a hug. "Tell Savannah I'll be over to visit after she goes home."

"I'll do that." After another long look at his baby daughter, Cruz ambled down the hall.

There were five babies in the nursery, and Violet looked from one to the other as a yearning gripped her heart.

Unexpectedly, she felt Peter's arm curve around her shoulders. "What are you thinking?" he asked.

"I'm thinking becoming a mother has to be an awesome experience."

"And?"

He already knew her so well. "And... I was thinking about the look on your face when you first saw the baby."

She and Peter had waited in the lounge while Cruz had coached his wife through labor. After the nurse had brought the baby to the nursery, she and Peter had taken their first looks.

"A baby's birth is a miraculous event, but not only infants need nurturing. Every child is precious."

"Don't you want to peer through the nursery glass someday at your baby?"

"Sure, I do. But if that doesn't happen, I can still be a dad."

The future was so uncertain. Violet wished she could see around the next corner. She wished she had that crystal ball. But standing here with Peter, his body close to hers, she knew she wanted him in her life. However, if she returned to New York and took Celeste with her, then what would happen?

Traveling in first class on Thursday morning, Violet glanced over at Ryan who was staring out the window. Peter was across the aisle, lost in a medical journal. They hadn't had much time together after the birth of Savannah and Cruz's baby. Peter had been paged while they were still at the hospital, and this morning was the first she had seen him since that night.

She'd visited Celeste before driving to the airport to explain that she and Peter would be away today and tomorrow. The child had looked up at her with worry in her dark brown eyes and asked, "But you'll be back?" Violet had solemnly promised that she and Peter would both be back, but Celeste's little arms had held on tight for a long while.

Now Violet tried to push thoughts of Celeste aside as concern for Ryan overtook everything else. She laid her hand on his. "How are you doing?"

"Holding my own," he said easily. "Wondering why I let Peter convince me to do this."

"You want a stab at a longer life."

"Maybe. But I have to wonder what that stab is going to cost me. If it means I'm going to be miserable and sick while I live longer…"

"You have to talk to the head of the program. Give this a chance, Ryan."

"I thought you were on *my* side."

"I am. I'll support you in whatever you choose. But you have to look at every option to make an informed decision, don't you think?"

"You've been hanging around Peter Clark

too long," he muttered as his hand went to his head and he rubbed his temple.

"Headache?"

"Yeah. A constant one."

"You've got to tell Lily about this."

"Lily's barely speaking to me right now. I'm not sure why. I don't think I did anything in particular to upset her, but when I walk into a room, she leaves. And she's always busy with something."

"Have you ever heard of women's intuition?"

Ryan managed to smile. "Sometime over the years somebody might have mentioned it."

"Don't scoff at it. She knows you're keeping something from her, and she probably has a short list of what she thinks that is. You need to tell her what's going on with you."

After a weary sigh, he concluded, "All in good time."

The problem was, Ryan might not have that much time. "Are you sure you don't want to stay at my apartment tonight?"

"So you and Peter can keep an eye on me? I don't think so."

He fished a piece of paper out of his jeans pocket. "I'll be at this address."

She glanced at the name. Clancy Flannery.

The address was only about ten blocks from her apartment. "A friend?"

"Yeah. An old one. We went to high school together. Clancy worked for Fortune TX, Ltd. way back when, but he always had his eye on the Big Apple, rather than staying in Red Rock. He joined an investment banking firm in New York and did well at it. Now he's retired. He travels quite a bit, but he's at home now. We have a lot of catching up to do."

"Are you going to tell him why you're here?"

"I might. Clancy knows how to keep his mouth shut. He's another contact in the city in case I decide to have treatment there. Then I won't have to rely just on your parents."

She knew Ryan didn't want to be a burden on anyone.

Suddenly there was a shout from coach class.

The flight attendant from first class hurried down the aisle as a voice came over the loudspeaker. "If there's a doctor on the plane, please identify yourself immediately. We have an emergency. "

Of one accord, both Violet and Peter rose from their seats and rushed toward the commotion in the rear of the plane. Two flight attendants were giving a man CPR, while a third came rushing from the back with a machine that looked no bigger than a briefcase.

"They have a portable defibrillator, thank God," Violet murmured. "He must be having a heart attack."

Seconds later, Peter had explained he was a doctor and so was Violet. He checked the patient's airway, breathing and pulse as Violet opened the box.

After switching on the device, she connected the electrode leads. Peter had the man's shirt opened and his chest was bare. Violet stuck two adhesive pads there containing the electrodes that functioned as ECG sensors to determine whether defibrillation was appropriate.

While Violet studied the digital readout, she saw that it was.

Peter said to everyone around, "Don't touch the patient." Then he nodded to Violet when he saw everyone was clear.

Without hesitating, she pressed the shock button. After the shock was completed, the device checked the cardiac rhythm and repeated it again.

Afterward, Peter checked the man's pulse. "Got one," he said with relief.

The patient was breathing again, and Violet

looked up at the flight attendant. "How much longer until we land?"

"I'll check with the pilot," she answered Violet.

Two minutes later she was back. "We've begun our descent, and we'll be on the ground in fifteen minutes. We've already called for an ambulance. Are you going to move him?"

Violet glanced at Peter and he shook his head. Although their position in the aisle was awkward, she answered, "Let's just keep him here. Do you know his name?"

"Sam Crawford. He's in public relations or something, and often takes this flight."

Peter capped the man's shoulder. "Hold on, Sam."

After that, time passed in a blur. She and Peter monitored Sam's condition until they were on the ground. All the passengers stayed in their seats as paramedics hooked the man up to an IV line, gave him oxygen and transported him from the plane. Then the other passengers began disembarking.

Once they were inside the terminal, the flight attendant rushed up to them. "A representative from the airline wants to thank you. You saved Mr. Crawford's life."

Peter exchanged a glance with Violet that

told her he didn't want the thanks or the acknowledgment. "Your crew started CPR. That was important. Having the defibrillator on board was what saved his life."

"Still," the flight attendant said, "Mr. Rossi wants to thank you personally. Here he comes now. I think that's Catherine Watson with Channel 6 News," she added in a murmur.

No one was supposed to know that Peter was with Violet and Ryan in New York. All they needed were pictures flashing across the news for Lily and the family to see before Ryan was ready to talk about his condition. And when the reporter learned Violet's name was Fortune...

Ryan had stepped to one side, and now Peter took Violet's hand. "I'm sorry. We can't stay to talk. We have an appointment."

Before the flight attendant could stop them or warn Rossi they were leaving, Peter, Violet and Ryan got themselves lost in the crowd.

With their carry-on luggage, they made their way to the exit. There was a driver there, holding up a sign for Clark.

Peter said to Ryan, "I thought you'd be more comfortable in a car than in a taxi."

Five minutes later, they were speeding toward the city. From the front seat, Ryan glanced over his shoulder at them. "You two work well together."

Peter leaned close to Violet and whispered only loud enough for her to hear, "That's not *all* we do well together."

The timbre of his voice as well as the intent in his words heated her all over. She thought about tonight and being alone with him in her apartment.

"Mr. Crawford is probably going to want to know who saved his life," Ryan went on.

"I'll call and see how he's doing when we have a few minutes. The flight attendant gave me the name of the hospital where he was taken."

Peter asked Ryan, "Are you going straight to your friend's, or do you want to go to dinner with Violet and me?"

"I promised Clancy I'd have dinner with him. He has a personal chef, so we won't even have to go out."

"Do you want us to pick you up in the morning?"

"No, I'll meet you at the hospital. It's not that I don't want your company," he said to Violet and Peter with a half smile, "but I'm mulling over lots of stuff—about the ranch, about Fortune TX, Ltd. Away from it, I'm hoping I'll find the answers more easily."

Her gaze met Peter's, and she saw sympathy there for the decisions Ryan might have to make.

They dropped off Ryan first, and then the driver took them to Violet's apartment building. After Peter paid the driver and collected their suitcases, the doorman opened the door for them. "Good evening, Dr. Fortune."

"Hi, Ralph. Any excitement while I was gone?"

"Nope. Not around here, anyway."

Violet's building was in the Upper West side, close to Central Park. She loved the old pre-war building, mainly because of its landscaped courtyard. She loved to go out there and sit under a tree.

After they took the elevator to the third floor, Violet unlocked her apartment door, and they went inside.

Peter had been quiet on the drive. Now as he studied her small living room, he looked as if he was trying to learn more about her by doing it. She watched his expression as his gaze passed over the windows that in the daytime let in lots of sunlight, over the blue-and-yellow plaid couch and matching yellow armchair, over the bookshelves, occasional tables and many mementoes scattered about. There was a carved oak table she'd found at a flea market and four chairs in its own cozy area for dining.

"What are you thinking?" she asked.

As his eyes passed over framed watercolors on the wall and peered into the tiny kitchen with its peach-and-white ceramic tile floor, he said, "I guess I expected something more luxurious."

"I didn't need it. I only have one bedroom because I rarely have guests over. If someone does stay over, the sofa pulls out into a sleeper. I've got to admit, I'm not here very much. I had fun furnishing and decorating it, and all of it is just comfortable for me."

Smiling, he stepped closer to her. "I like it."

He'd dropped their luggage inside the door. Now he stood about six inches from her, his green eyes glimmering, no doubt with the thoughts that were running through her head, too.

"What do you want to do first?" Her words came out bumpy and thready. He only had to get this close and she was trembling.

Slipping his hands under her hair, he gently pulled her toward him. "What about a walk?"

It wasn't what she was expecting, and her disappointment must have shown.

He chuckled. "I just wanted to see your reaction," he teased and tilted her face up to his.

All thoughts of the future were forgotten and she realized she'd just put it on hold. Nothing mattered more right now than Peter's hands on her skin, his body so close to hers.

"I want you," he growled, and the deep huskiness of his voice, the wonderful, tantalizing sensation of his touch made her mouth too dry to speak. So, instead of speaking, her hands went to his shoulders and she hung on, ready for a ride.

When Peter's tongue slipped along her lips, she responded by opening to him. As he thrust inside, she felt completion, even in this small way, knowing she'd feel even more complete when they truly joined their bodies. With greedy fervor, he stroked her tongue and she became dizzy with the passion between them, overwhelmed by her feelings for him. Yet she knew those feelings, without action, would mean nothing to Peter.

They didn't even make it to her bedroom. The kiss detonated their desire and they began unbuttoning, unfastening and tearing clothes away.

Peter's kisses became hungrier, more possessive, more claiming, until she cared about noth-

ing but him. The desire between them became
almost too hot to handle and her breathing became as ragged as his. Her slacks dropped to
the floor. While she stepped out of them, he
unbuckled his belt, his gaze staying on hers,
connecting them. She gravitated toward him,
putting her hands on his waist, sliding her
hands up into his chest hair, ridging his nipples with her tongue. When he shuddered, she
gloried in that.

Before, they'd bantered during their love-
making. Now there was complete seriousness in everything they did. When they were
both finally naked, he caught her to him, and
she wrapped her arms around his neck. As he
lifted her up against him, she wrapped her legs
around him.

"Peter," she sighed, wanting so much she
couldn't even put the wanting into words.

"I know," he murmured, grabbing one of the
chairs from the table. He turned it around, then
sat on it with her facing him.

"I need you, Violet." There was something in
his voice that told her he'd never told a woman
that before.

"I need you, too," she whispered.

His hands on her bottom, he lifted her and
let her slide onto him…slowly. Pleasure rushed

through her. As he thrust upward, she held on for dear life.

"I can't hold out much longer," he admitted in a rocky voice. "Are you ready?"

The pleasure was building into a firestorm in her womb. She knew one more stroke and—

"I'm ready," she gasped.

When he pushed into her more forcefully, her climax encompassed her, shaking her, making her limbs tremble, forcing her to see that her love for Peter was bigger than anything else in her life.

A small voice asked, *Bigger than Celeste?*

In the maelstrom of sensation and emotion and absolute pleasure she couldn't answer the question. She couldn't consider the repercussions.

Tonight she needed to take time out from the real world. Tonight she wanted to just love Peter and not think about anything else. Holding on to him, she let wave after wave of physical pleasure wash over her. Emotions rose up until tears fell down her cheeks. As Peter's release came, too, she felt him shudder…felt him hold on to her tighter…felt the bond between them strengthen.

Seconds later he rested his forehead against hers. "We were very foolish tonight."

Surprised, Violet leaned back a little. "Why?"

"Because we didn't use protection. We're both doctors, and old enough to know better, yet we still behaved like teenagers."

"I told you getting pregnant wouldn't be easy for me. But if it happens, we'll deal with it." As she said the words, she wondered if she *wanted* to get pregnant and that was why she'd ignored birth control. Maybe that was Peter's reason, too.

Now he slid his thumb under her chin and just studied her. She knew he was going to ask questions. She knew he wanted answers. She still didn't have them.

So before he could even open his lips, she put her finger on them. "For tonight...for just this one night, can we pretend we don't have any cares in the world? Can we just be Peter and Violet in New York? Being together without worrying about tomorrow?"

"Can you really put tomorrow out of your head?"

"Yes. We need tonight to give us strength for what comes after. Whatever that is."

Tenderly, he passed his hand up and down her bare back. "All right. We'll try it. I've never suspended reality before. What do you want to do next?"

"Let's walk the streets a bit. I'll show you where we can get a great bottle of wine and then a corner market where we can buy hot food for takeout. I'll show you all the things I like best about New York."

"In the next few hours?" he asked wryly.

"I'll do my best. It's the sights and the sounds and the smells as much as anything else."

"I'm game. But first—"

He bent his head to kiss her again, and Violet couldn't remember ever feeling this happy before.

Autumn in New York was one of Violet's favorite times. She loved the crisp nip of the end-of-October air, the expectancy that the city would even be busier for the holidays, and the leaves in Central Park that turned golden and orange and red. She gave Peter a taste of all of it—from street vendors to newsstands to window-shopping. In his hunter-green cable knit sweater and black corduroys, he turned women's heads as he walked by. But he kept his arm around *her* during most of their walk, even taking her hand now and then. She felt as if she belonged with him and wasn't sure why that made her feel so good.

Peter asked if she'd like to go to a restaurant

to eat, but she preferred picking up the bits and pieces of their meal and taking it all back to her apartment with him. It was cozier there, and a lot more intimate than having people talking all around them and a waiter interrupting their conversation.

Together, they chose a bottle of Merlot, then stopped at a corner market, filling their basket with a loaf of French bread, fruit and a few entrées from the hot buffet bar. Her apartment wasn't far away, and ten minutes later they were taking the elevator, then tumbling into her living room laughing at a joke he'd made, and kissing, in spite of the bags in their arms.

After they'd taken everything out of the bags and opened the many containers, Peter poured the wine into two stemmed glasses.

Violet was placing plates and silverware on the table when her phone rang. She took her cell phone from her purse. "Hello."

"Violet, it's Miles."

"Miles, hi. Are you checking up on me for Clyde?"

He gave a short laugh. "No way. I know better. I thought I'd better forewarn you about something."

"What?"

"A story broke in today's *Gazette*."

"A story about what?"

"About Kingston Fortune and where he came from."

"Exactly what about Kingston?"

"Everything. The fact that he was illegitimate...that his biological parents were Eliza Wise and Travis Jamison, not Dora and Hobart Fortune."

"Who do you suppose talked?"

"It could have been anybody. The police know, the family knows. Somebody might have gotten friendly with a reporter and revealed it without intending to." His voice lowered as he said, "Or someone could have gotten hold of the information and spilled it to embarrass Ryan."

Ryan. Had Lily called him? He didn't need anything more to worry about, including embarrassment for his family—if there *was* any embarrassment in being the son of a man who was given away by a mother who didn't want him.

"The story being let out of the bag might not be a bad thing," she told her brother. "Maybe now everyone will stop speculating on why Christopher Jamison had a crown birthmark."

"Maybe. Or maybe it will make matters worse. We'll know in a few days. But I just wanted to warn you in case any reporters bothered *you*."

"No one has my cell phone number but family or friends, and I can screen calls on my machine."

"When will you be back?"

"Hopefully, tomorrow evening. Don't worry about me, Miles. I'm a big girl."

"That's *why* I worry," he grumbled in a wry tone. "You take care, and don't get run over by a taxi."

She laughed. "I won't. I'll talk to you soon."

After she dropped her phone back into her purse, Peter asked, "Trouble?"

"Maybe. Maybe not. There was an article in the Red Rock paper this morning about the Fortune family."

Peter motioned to the food at the table. "Come on. Sit and eat before it gets cold, and you can tell me about it."

They dug into the containers, and when their plates were full she began, "Kingston Fortune wasn't really a Fortune."

Peter's eyebrows arched. "Who was he?"

"His biological father was a man named Travis Jamison."

"Any relation to Christopher Jamison?"

"Oh, yes. Christopher would have been his

great-grandson. But from what I understand, Travis never knew he *had* a son."

"This is going to get complicated, isn't it?" Peter asked with a smile.

"Yes, it is. But the bottom line is, Travis got a young girl pregnant, and she didn't tell him about the child. Since she didn't want the baby, she handed him off to a family in another county—the Fortunes. That baby was Kingston, Ryan's father."

"And all of this is just coming out?"

"Ryan found out about it when Christopher Jamison's body was identified. He found out about the whole Jamison history."

"Interesting. Is this the reason that the police still have their sights set on Ryan?"

"I imagine it's one of them, though Ryan knew nothing about the history before the body was discovered."

"Now all that will be made public, so the whole state can speculate."

She nodded.

Silence dwindled into easy companionship. But in that ease, an underlying current of sexual tension rose. When Violet looked at Peter, all she could think of was how he'd made love to her. From the way he looked back, he was thinking about the same thing.

Their conversation turned to other things then, interesting items from their past. It was light talk, about plays they'd seen, places they'd been, things they'd done.

Finally Peter pushed back his plate. "That food was delicious. Do you do that often? Go there for supper?"

"Once in a great while. I try to resist. Usually I buy salads and fruit," she responded. "Remember that yogurt and black coffee? I never really learned how to cook."

"I know what you mean. Once in a while, Charlene and my sisters bring over casseroles. The rest of the time I subsist on burgers, frozen French fries and microwave meals or fast food."

"And we're doctors!" Violet said with a laugh.

"Yes, we are," Peter agreed.

So as not to go down that conversational path, Violet hopped up and began to clear the table. "I think I'd like to get a shower before I turn in. Can I get you anything else first? There's ice cream in the freezer."

"I think I'll pass on the ice cream for now. Maybe later. I'll catch up on the day's events on the news channel while you shower."

She wasn't going to ask what they were going to do after she showered. But she could hope.

Violet had just soaped her hair, picturing her and Peter sharing ice cream and kisses in her bed, when a tap on the shower door made her jump.

When Peter opened the frosted glass door, he was naked. "I thought you might need help soaping hard-to-reach places." The amusement in his eyes, as well as his suggestive tone, was irresistible.

"My shower isn't very big," she breathed, getting tingly all over from just thinking about his suggestion.

He looked around the small space. "I think we'll both fit. It's your call."

"Come—" She couldn't seem to find her voice, cleared her throat and tried again. "Come on in."

His green gaze was filled with desire.

Her hand went through her hair. "I'm still all soapy."

"We'll take care of that." Then he closed the door and was standing so close, their bodies brushed. "Did you wash yet?"

She shook her head, feeling strangely embarrassed, even though they'd already made love twice.

"What's the matter?" he asked.

"I don't know. I guess I'm just not used to this kind of intimacy."

"Do you want my hands on you?"

The question almost derailed all of her thoughts, but she looked up at him and managed to say, "Yes."

Her net ball was hanging on one of the spigots. He lifted it off, took the body wash from the shelf and dribbled some of the liquid onto the net. Then he took it in his hands and rubbed it up and down her arms until the suds overflowed through the net. With suds in his hands, he cupped her breasts. The soap and the water and the slide of his fingers almost made her crazy. His touches weren't quite sexual, yet they weren't completely utilitarian, either. His hands were large, and as his fingers slid over her stomach, around her sides and up her back, she thought she was going to swoon. Steam billowed around them and she knew it wasn't coming just from the hot water.

Stepping closer, his hand slid down her back to her buttocks and played there.

"Peter," she breathed.

"What?"

"You make me feel so...wanton."

"Then I'm doing something right."

He squeezed more suds from the ball into

one hand, then hung it on the spigot with his other. His chest hair teased her nipples, and his arousal pressed against her belly. Then his hand was between her legs, soapy and slick and seductive. She'd never felt anything like it—Peter's pure, sensual attention to her...his desire to make them both delirious with wanting... the closeness of two lovers sharing the same shower. When his fingers slid into her, she felt as if she was going to come apart.

"You," she said as the water swished down on them. "I want you inside of me."

"Can't I do this first?" he teased as her body contracted around his finger and she felt the first orgasm. The tension inside of her wasn't nearly dissipated. He moved his finger again and touched his thumb to the nub that gave her the most pleasure.

"Peter," she cried as she hung on to his shoulders and let the sensual magic take over.

"I'm here," he assured her, and then he was as he lifted her and thrust into her. Pressing her back against the wall of the shower, he admitted in a husky voice, "I've never even thought about doing this before."

Time stopped. The world spun. Their pleasure-filled sounds echoed against the shower walls. When Violet's body contracted around

Peter, he let his own release come. His mouth covered hers, and as he pulsed into her repeatedly, she knew she'd never love a man this way again. They held each other as their bodies trembled, and eventually their breathing slowed. When she loosened her legs, Peter let her back down onto her feet.

"Wow!" she said, smiling up at him.

"Double wow!" he agreed, nipping her neck with his lips, kissing her chin and finally leaning slightly away.

"Do you think we'll ever do this like a normal couple? In a bed?"

His laughter rumbled around them. Then he held her face between his hands. "As soon as we get dried off, maybe have some ice cream, I could arrange that. Unless you intended for me to sleep on your sofa."

She shook her head. "I want to feel your arms around me all night."

When he kissed her again, she knew reality would probably clobber them in the morning. But for tonight, she wanted the fantasy. She wanted Peter.

And maybe, if they were lucky, they could carry some of the fantasy with them into the morning.

Chapter 12

The hospital was a maze of corridors, rooms, offices and operating suites. After meeting Ryan at the information desk, Violet and Peter led him to the elevator that took them to the tenth floor. Dr. Hanneken's office was located there. He was the doctor in charge of the program Ryan might be participating in.

Everything about the atmosphere here was clinical—from the highly polished gray-tiled floor to the pale gray walls, long fluorescent lights and vinyl chairs. Ryan had been rubbing his forehead all morning, and Violet knew that meant he had a headache.

After he checked in with the receptionist and

the three of them settled in those hard, vinyl chairs, Violet asked, "Did you get any sleep last night?"

"Are you kidding? Thinking about these trials and what they might want to do to me is bad enough. But then I got a call from Lily."

"About the article in the *Red Rock Gazette?*"

"So you got a call, too?" he asked, his brows raised.

"Miles wanted to warn me. But I have to ask—is it so bad that the truth is out?"

After Ryan looked down at his boots, shifted one out in front of the other, his gaze met Peter's. "Do you know what she's talking about?"

"Violet filled me in last night."

Peter's arm brushed Violet's as he leaned forward to address Ryan. He was wearing a beige oxford shirt this morning with black corduroy slacks. With his shirt collar open and his sleeves rolled back to his forearms he looked *so* sexy.

Violet remembered absolutely every second of their night together. After their exciting encounter in the shower, she'd soaped and washed Peter, thoroughly arousing him all over again. But he'd slowed everything down. They'd rinsed, toweled off each other unhurriedly and gone to the kitchen for ice cream.

However, after they'd brought dishes of it to bed, they'd only eaten a few spoonfuls when they'd decided to taste the ice cream from each other's lips. The dessert melted as the heat they generated in the bed almost lit up the room.

This morning she should be tired, but she wasn't. They'd arisen early, kissed often, gone for bagels and coffee, then taken a taxi to the hospital. She'd called Celeste from the lobby and both she and Peter had talked to her, simply to let the little girl know they were thinking about her.

Now Peter asked Ryan, "Was Lily upset about the article?"

"Lily's *been* upset. This article didn't help. Maybe tonight I'll be able to call her and invite her up here with me. Then I can lay everything out on the table and we can really talk. She'll have to know if I'm going to be part of these trials."

"You sound as if you might be prepared to go through treatment."

"If I'm not, I'm sure Lily will convince me."

Unable to suppress her smile, Violet knew Ryan was right about that. Lily was a scrapper, and if she had any say in this, she'd have him fight this tumor to his dying breath.

Obviously restless, Ryan stood, paced a

while, then came back to stand before them. Addressing Peter, he asked, "If I take part in these trials, do I get any breaks? I mean…will I be able to go home at all?"

"You're going to have to wait and ask the doctor that," Peter answered.

"If I can't go home, there's going to be some awfully disappointed people, including your brother," Ryan said to Violet. "Steven's been working hard to get his ranch ready for that party the governor's going to attend. If I can't be there, I'll screw up everyone's plans. Steven and Amy will be disappointed."

"They won't be upset once they know what's going on," Violet assured him. "And neither will anyone else. Your health comes first."

"What about the governor?" Ryan went on. "They fit the event into his schedule."

"You're trying to cross too many bridges," Peter said kindly.

"I can't stop my mind from racing," Ryan admitted.

Knowing that phenomenon all too well, Violet asked him, "Did you make a list of all your questions?"

He patted his jeans pocket. "Yep. They're in here."

Blowing out a breath again, he stared at the

receptionist, as if by doing so he could make her call his name. But she just kept on working.

Finally, he sighed and sat down once more. "Did you two find anything out about that man you helped on the plane?"

"I called this morning to check on him," Violet said. "The nurse wouldn't give me any information at first, but after I told her who I was, she connected me to the chief of staff. I think he just wanted to verify my name. He said he'd have to check with the Crawford family before releasing any information. Five minutes later he called me back to tell me Mr. Crawford was stable."

"You might end up as a story in the *New York Times*," Ryan responded wryly.

"I don't think so. The chief of staff promised to respect our privacy."

After Ryan checked his watch for the tenth time he grumbled, "How much longer do you think it's going to be? We've already been waiting fifteen minutes."

"There's no way of knowing," Violet answered, cognizant of doctors and their schedules.

Obviously not used to inaction himself, Peter stood. "I'll go get us some coffee."

After Peter returned, they drank their coffee then waited some more. An hour later, two men in lab coats rushed in and Violet couldn't tell if they were doctors or not. They were moving too fast for her to read their name tags. The phone on the receptionist's desk began ringing incessantly. A brunette who looked to be in her forties also raced in, a sheaf of papers in her hand. She looked worried, upset and altogether frazzled. Rather than stopping at the receptionist, she opened the door to the examination rooms, then went down that corridor.

"I wonder what's going on," Ryan mumbled.

"It could have something to do with our wait," Peter said.

Fifteen minutes after that, Violet checked with the receptionist. She honestly said she wasn't sure how much longer it would be, and she couldn't check with the doctor right now. Without further explanation, she asked Violet to please be patient.

Another hour later, Ryan had taken several walks down the outside hall and was beyond patience. Violet couldn't blame him, but she knew all too well that at times this is the way doctors and hospitals and appointments worked.

Finally, a doctor with thinning black hair entered the waiting area. His name tag read

Dr. Doug Hanneken, the physician with whom Ryan was supposed to consult. Spotting them, the doctor frowned, then approached and greeted them solemnly. "Mr. Fortune?" he asked, targeting Ryan whose Stetson as well as his age gave away his identity.

"I was about ready to walk out," Ryan said angrily.

"This delay this morning couldn't be helped. And it directly affects you, I'm afraid."

Violet didn't like the sound of that. With a glance at Peter, she saw he didn't, either.

"Come back to my office with me," Dr. Hanneken directed, hurrying toward the door that led to the examination rooms, expecting Ryan to follow. They all followed.

Moments later, they were sitting in the doctor's office. Perched on the corner of his desk, Dr. Hanneken rubbed his hand across his brow, and Violet realized he looked as if he hadn't had much sleep.

Finally he addressed Ryan. "I'm sorry to have to tell you this, but one of the clinical trial patients died this morning, possibly as a result of the experimental drugs. The trials are being shut down until we can investigate further. So, I'm sorry to say, you're going to have to look elsewhere for a program that might help you."

Stunned silence met his words until Peter sat forward in his chair. "Can you make any recommendations for other programs?"

"There aren't others here. I'll have to do some checking. I simply don't have time for that right now. I hope you understand, but this is a catastrophe for us."

Violet knew Peter understood, and *she* understood. But she wasn't sure Ryan would.

He looked shell-shocked. But then a calm expression settled on his face and he stood. "Okay, Doc. That's that. It's meant to be."

"It's *not* meant to be," Peter protested. "You can have chemo and radiation to keep you alive until you can get into another program."

"No. No chemo. No radiation. No program. This just reinforces what I've felt all along. I want to go home to Texas and Lily. I want to live out my last months with her in peace. I don't know when I'm going to tell her, and I want you two to keep my confidence."

After a moment of hesitation, Violet murmured, "You know we will."

"Peter?" Ryan asked.

"You know I will. But I still think you're wrong about all of it. Lily could be standing beside you, helping you, supporting you."

"She will be, in a little while. I have things to get in order before this goes public."

Unable to keep tears from filling her eyes, Violet blinked them away. She'd been so hopeful for Ryan, and she knew Peter had been, too. Now...

Dr. Hanneken went around to the back of his desk. "If you need more time to talk about this—"

"I don't need any more time to talk," Ryan interrupted him, resignation in his voice. To Peter and Violet he said, "Let's see if we can get a flight out of here today."

But Peter wasn't going to let go yet. "Let's go back to Violet's apartment. I'll make some calls."

Shaking his head, Ryan capped Peter's shoulder. "Look, son, I know this is hard for you to accept. I appreciate everything you've done for me. I do. But now it's time to let me deal with it."

"You have to have a local doctor—"

Ryan cut in. "I know. And I will in good time. For now I just want to go home."

As Ryan headed for the door and out of Dr. Hanneken's office, Peter dropped his arm around Violet's shoulders, thanked the physician, then led her out into the short hall. Ryan was already in the waiting room.

"I'll make him listen to me," Peter said.

"You can only do so much. This is Ryan's life. What's left of it. It's up to him now." Although Violet was wrapped up in worry for Ryan, she realized he wanted to return to Texas to put his life in order. She suddenly understood she needed to put her life in order, too. There was something she needed to do before she left the city. "I have a few things to take care of before we return to Red Rock. Can you keep Ryan company this afternoon while I go into my office?"

"Sure, if he'll let me. I'll try to book us on the last flight out tonight."

Then Peter pulled her tight into his body for a hug, for support, for comfort. They both needed it. With a flush of insight, Violet realized that this was what loving someone was all about. Maybe if she went to her office, she'd figure out how to make a relationship with Peter work. She'd figure out how much her career meant to her, and what she was willing to give up to be with him.

The physicians with whom Violet shared office space greeted her as if she'd never been away. The receptionist told her there was a stack of nonurgent messages on her desk. After a few moments of chitchat, Violet headed that way.

When she stepped into her office, she closed the door, not feeling the sense of homecoming she usually felt. Glimpsing the pink slips on the desk, she went to them and picked up the stack. There were about fifteen. She studied each one, realizing they were messages from friends or acquaintances who hadn't been able to reach her at her apartment. She stuffed the pink slips into her purse, intending to make the calls from Red Rock after she got back.

When she sat at her desk, she saw the folder. It was positioned on the back corner. Anne Washburn's records.

Still shaken up about Ryan, knowing his decision not to have treatment was his final one, she blinked away quick tears. She would help make Ryan's last days as happy for him as she could. She would cherish the bond they shared and let him lean on her if he wanted to. Maybe the doctors were wrong and the six months they'd given him would stretch much longer.

Slowly reaching for Anne Washburn's folder, Violet opened it and began reading. She went over every word, every line, until there were no more lines to read. Then she picked up the phone. Carl Washburn owned a restaurant and had an erratic schedule. If she couldn't get hold of him at home, maybe she could catch him at work.

When the phone rang for the fifth time, she almost gave up hope. But then he answered. "Hello."

His voice sounded tired, his soul weary, and she didn't want to add to the burden of losing his wife and child. "Mr. Washburn, it's Dr. Fortune."

There was cold silence until finally he asked, "Why are you calling?"

"I'm calling because you and Anne and the baby have been on my mind."

The line went quiet again.

"I just wanted to tell you that Anne wasn't simply another patient to me," Violet went on. "She wasn't merely a number."

When he still didn't speak, Violet knew this had been a mistake. "I'm sorry to intrude on your grief. I shouldn't have called."

She was about to say goodbye when Carl Washburn murmured, "I thought about calling you." His voice was clipped from the emotion in it.

"What did you want to talk to me about?"

After a short pause, he cleared his throat. "I'm sorry for the things I said. I consulted a lawyer. I didn't know what else to do with my pain. But after a few days he called me into his office for a meeting and looked me straight in the eye. He told me he'd done some checking and there was nothing negligent about the way you or Dr. Owens handled the case. I knew that all along. I just didn't want to admit it. I was trying to find somebody to blame."

"Mr. Washburn, I can't tell you I understand your loss. I've never lost a spouse. But I was pregnant when I was young, and that ended badly. When someone dies, our dreams die with them. It seems our future dies with them, too."

"Yeah. That's it exactly. I couldn't figure out why I was supposed to get up in the morning anymore. I wanted explanations and I couldn't find any."

"I explained the best I could—"

Rapidly he cut in. "Oh, I don't mean medical explanations. I mean the *big* explanation. You know. Why it happened. Why I'm still here and they're not."

"I know," she murmured, understanding his confusion. "How are you doing now?"

"My sister made me go for grief counseling.

She practically hog-tied me to get me there. I still don't want to go, but I think it's helping."

"Good. I'm glad."

"I don't blame you," he blurted out, as if it was hard for him to say. "I know you advised Anne to have surgery because that was the best thing for her. I also know if she hadn't had surgery, what happened on the operating table could have happened anytime."

Violet had tried to explain that to Carl after Anne's death, but he hadn't been ready to listen. "I'm glad you found support. I know it doesn't seem like it now, but the passing of time will help."

"Yeah, I know. That's what everybody tells me. A year from now I'll let you know if it's true." He paused. "My lawyer told me you were out of town on vacation or something. Was that because of Anne?"

The man was perceptive. "Yes, it was."

"I'm glad you called, Dr. Fortune."

"I'm glad I called, too. Take care of yourself, Mr. Washburn."

"I will. I know Anne would want me to. I know she'd want me to get on with my life, and eventually I'll do that."

After an exchange of goodbyes, Violet hung up the phone. She glanced at Anne Washburn's file one more time. Then she closed it and took it out to the receptionist for her to file, feeling more peaceful than she had in a very long time.

On Saturday evening, Violet turned down the vegetables on the stove, not at all sure of what she was doing. Last night, when she and Peter and Ryan had returned to Red Rock, Peter had gone straight to the hospital and she had dropped off Ryan at the Double Crown. Saying goodbye to him had been tough. All she could do was hug him and tell him to call her if he needed her. As she'd driven away, she hoped that he would. She hoped he would tell Lily soon what was happening to him.

Whenever Violet thought about losing Ryan, the sadness that filled her seemed overwhelming. So after leaving the Double Crown, she'd stopped to see Celeste. The little girl had obviously missed her, and Violet had tucked her in for the night, staying until she fell asleep. At home afterward, she had been getting ready for bed herself when Peter called.

"Hey," he'd said in an intimate, sexy voice that had taken her back to her apartment in New York and everything they'd done together.

"Hey, yourself. Are you finished at the hospital?"

"Nope. Not yet. But I knew you'd be going to bed soon. How about dinner tomorrow night?"

"Are you on call?"

"Nope. Where would you like to go?"

"Why don't you come here? I'll cook."

His voice held amusement. "You'll cook?"

"Just because I haven't had much time to do it doesn't mean I *can't* do it. I can read. Unless you're not willing to take a chance."

In the few seconds before he spoke, she realized her statement held more than one meaning.

"All right," Peter said. "I'll take a chance. What time?"

"Can you get away by seven?"

"Seven's good. I'll see you then. And, Violet?"

"Yes?" she whispered.

"Imagine me kissing you good-night."

"I will."

Now, as she remembered the conversation and the anticipatory excitement that had kept her awake much of the night, she scurried around the pool house, wanting dinner to be perfect. How difficult could it be to serve a meal?

She found out. At seven-thirty Peter called to tell her he was on his way. He'd gotten tied up with a consultation. Taking another peek at the roast in the oven at eight, she finally heard the sound of tires on the gravel outside and heaved a sigh of relief.

Her relief was short-lived, however. When she removed the roast beef from the oven she noticed all of the broth had cooked away and the meat was overdone and dry. The carrots and string beans she'd steamed on top of the stove were soggy and limp. Only the baked potatoes had survived. After all, what could go wrong with baked potatoes?

Peter knocked, but didn't wait for her to answer before he came in, a bag in each hand. When he found her in the kitchen area, he set the bags on the counter. "I'm sorry about the delay."

She knew he was. She also knew in their profession, delays were commonplace. She should have allowed for the possibility he'd be late.

Glumly she looked up at him. "It's a good thing I picked up a loaf of bread at the bakery because the rest of dinner is a disaster."

The roast was sitting on a dish on the counter. Peter poked it with the fork that had been lying beside it. "Hmm. Looks like I'll get a lot of exercise chewing."

"You don't need teeth for the vegetables," she warned him.

Grinning, he took her into his arms. "Any

food is good food after the day I've had. I brought a bottle of wine since I'm not on call tonight. And..."

He retrieved one of the bags he'd set on the counter. "How about chocolate-covered strawberries for dessert?"

He was being such a sport about this, and she should be, too. "You don't have to eat the beef and vegetables," she said softly.

"If I kiss you right now, we won't be eating anything for a couple of hours anyway."

Peter was acting as if the meal didn't matter. Yet she knew he wanted a woman who could make a home. She'd never thought of herself as a homemaker.

He must have seen the doubt in her eyes. He must have seen the worry that somehow she wasn't measuring up.

Taking her chin in his hand, he muttered, "The hell with food," then he kissed her thoroughly.

She needed his kiss. She needed *him*. Last night, as she'd slept alone, she'd wanted Peter beside her. She'd wanted to be in his arms. She'd wanted to be giving him pleasure and receiving it. She'd wanted to love him and have that love returned. Whether she was being wise or foolish, she was weaving dreams about the two of them—she just hadn't ironed out the details.

When she laced her hands through his hair and pulled his head down for another kiss, he groaned. Not letting her get the upper hand, he tunneled his fingers under the hem of her sweater and was ready to raise it up and over her head when a Samba melody started playing from Violet's purse, which was lying on the counter.

"Do you have to get it?" he grumbled.

"I'd better. My service in New York has the number."

Reluctantly, Peter released her sweater. But he gave her another hungry kiss before she went to the counter.

Opening her purse, she retrieved her little blue phone. "Violet Fortune here."

"Dr. Fortune, this is Mrs. Crawford. You don't know me, but you saved my husband's life."

Violet turned the name over in her mind, repeated it aloud, then heard Peter say, "Flight to New York."

The man who had benefitted from the defibrillator on the airplane. "Oh, hello, Mrs. Crawford. How *is* your husband?"

"Glad to be alive. He's supposed to be released from the hospital tomorrow. I told him he should call you himself, but he felt funny about the way we got your number."

"How *did* you get it?"

She hesitated a moment. "I have a relative who's on the police force. He got it for me. He has his sources. I had another number and tried that first, but no one answered. I didn't want to just leave a message."

"I'm glad you called to let me know how your husband is doing."

"We wanted to thank Dr. Clark, too, but we didn't know how to trace him."

"He happens to be here. Would you like to speak to him?"

"Oh, yes. Please."

Violet handed off the phone to Peter, and for a few minutes he listened to Mrs. Crawford's thanks. "You tell your husband that he's supposed to listen to everything you tell him."

Whatever Mrs. Crawford said made Peter laugh out loud. "Yes, men can be a little stubborn. But so can women. I want you to know the flight attendants who did CPR on your husband saved his life, too."

After Peter listened for a few more moments, he said, "I'm sure they appreciated that. Maybe we'll stop in the next time we get to New York. No, we're not there now. I practice in Texas."

After he listened a little longer, he responded, "I'll relay that to Dr. Fortune. You and your husband take care."

When he closed Violet's phone, he smiled at her. "Mrs. Crawford owns Vintage And More—a shop that sells old clothes. She says the next time you're in New York you should stop in and pick out an outfit for yourself."

A sweet warmth filled Violet's heart. "Did she say you could do that, too?"

"Hardly. Though she said if I stop in, she always has imported chocolate in her shop, too. She sent the flight attendants flowers. I think she needs to thank us in some tangible way."

"That's kind of her."

Snatching up the bag that contained the chocolate-covered strawberries, he took Violet's hand and tugged her toward the bedroom.

"What are you doing?" she asked with a laugh.

"We're going to satisfy two appetites at once. Then maybe we can salvage some roast beef sandwiches out of dinner."

As soon as he pulled her down onto the bed beside him, she didn't care about roast beef sandwiches. She only cared about loving him right now.

Chapter 13

When Violet went to the rehab center on Monday, she checked her watch and saw Celeste would still be working with her morning therapists. Afterward they'd have lunch together, and play with the electronic game Peter had brought her yesterday.

Knowing Celeste's schedule by heart, Violet headed for the physical therapy room. When she stepped inside, the brightness of it made her smile. It was painted in primary colors—yellow walls with bright blue and red stripes halfway up. Above those, children could search out pictures of Winnie-the-Pooh, Cinderella and Nemo. The therapist had told her the large thick decals were removable and that they could always keep up-to-date with the children's favorite characters.

Violet spotted Celeste on a low, wide, padded table, where she was stretched out full-length. Her therapist was bending her leg up and down.

Violet tried never to interrupt Celeste's therapies. She observed, made notes in her head and waited until the therapists were finished.

Today the therapist looked up with a big smile. "She's doing great. Give us twenty minutes and we'll be finished."

Crossing over to Celeste, Violet brushed the girl's bangs from her forehead, gave her a thumbs-up sign and said, "I'll be back in a little while."

To Violet's surprise the therapist said to Celeste, "I'll be right back," and pulled Violet aside. In a low voice she murmured, "Celeste's social worker is here. I told her you usually came in around this time. She's waiting in the cafeteria."

"She wants to see me?"

"Yes. I'm not sure what it's all about, but she had papers in her hand and was talking to the director here this morning."

Violet didn't like the sound of that. "Okay.

I'll go find her. Her name is Mrs. Gunthry, right?"

The therapist nodded.

As Violet's heart tripped a little faster, she walked down the hall with its Dalmatian murals and entered the cafeteria. Mrs. Gunthry—Peter had once described her as a woman in her fifties with brown curly hair and tortoise-shell glasses—was the only person in the room, seated at a table, nursing a cup of coffee. She did, indeed, have a file folder in front of her, and she was making notes.

Approaching her, Violet stopped at her table. "Mrs. Gunthry?"

"Yes."

"I'm Violet Fortune. Celeste's therapist said you wanted to see me."

"Yes, I did. I've already called Dr. Clark. He's hoping to meet me here in a little while. I have to get an accurate status report on Celeste's condition."

"Why is that?"

Mrs. Gunthry pushed her glasses higher on her nose. "I know you've been visiting Celeste regularly, and Dr. Clark is monitoring her care. We've had an unexpected development in her case."

Violet waited.

"Dr. Clark probably mentioned that after her parents' accident we contacted a great-aunt who lives in Ohio."

"Yes, he mentioned it. She's older and said she didn't want a child."

"Yes, that was the case then. That's why Celeste went into foster care. But now, with her progress and the necessity of placing her again when she leaves Tumbleweed, we contacted the great-aunt once more."

"And?" Violet prompted.

After straightening a few of the papers, Mrs. Gunthry's gaze finally met Violet's. "I think she feels responsible for what happened to Celeste because of being placed in foster care. She told us that if Celeste is ambulatory and fully capable of taking care of herself by the time rehab is finished, she will take her."

"What do you mean, fully able to take care of herself? She's six!"

"Dr. Fortune, I think you know what that means. If she can dress herself, go to the bathroom herself, bathe herself. Apparently this aunt has arthritis and can't race after a child. That's understandable. But at least Celeste will have a place to go."

At least Celeste will have a place to go.

Violet's heart hurt at the thought of it. She

hated the idea that Celeste would be in the care of woman who, from the sound of it, might not really want her, but might eventually expect Celeste to take care of *her*.

"Did you speak to this aunt personally?" she asked.

"Yes, I did."

"What does your intuition tell you about her? Why does she want Celeste to come live with her?"

Looking uncomfortable, Mrs. Gunthry shifted in her chair. "She's in her sixties. My sense of it is, as Celeste gets older, she'll be able to do more things for her aunt."

No! Violet thought. *That is not a good reason to adopt a child.*

Before Violet could voice her concern, Mrs. Gunthry hurried on, "We have countless children who need homes, and not enough foster parents. When a relative agrees to take responsibility, we have to honor that."

Violet wanted to shout, *What if I agreed to adopt Celeste?*

But before those words came out of her mouth, she had to be absolutely sure that was what she wanted to do. She had to be absolutely sure she was ready for that change in her life.

"How soon is all this going to happen?"

"That's why I want to talk to Dr. Clark. I'm hoping he can give me a prognosis for Celeste and a tentative release date."

Again, Violet glanced at the papers spread before the social worker. "How long will you be here?"

"I'm going to wait for Dr. Clark, and then we'll have to conference." The woman checked her watch. "I'd say until one o'clock. I can't stay much past that. I have other cases and other work I have to be doing. I know that might seem callous to you, but Celeste is one of many."

In more turmoil than she could ever remember being in, Violet said, "Thank you for telling me all of this."

Turning and leaving the cafeteria, she headed out for some fresh air. She needed to clear her head. She needed to make some decisions. Now.

Peter strode quickly down the hall to Tumbleweed's cafeteria. When he saw Mrs. Gunthry, he frowned. He had about a half hour until he had to return to the hospital for a meeting. He didn't like mystery, but the social worker hadn't wanted to discuss anything over the phone.

Checking his watch again, he realized Violet

was probably having lunch with Celeste. His heart lightened at the thought. He missed Violet when he wasn't with her. It was a totally odd sensation for him. He'd never missed anyone like that. When they made love, his world seemed to tumble over itself. Yet when he held her afterward, he felt he could conquer anything. Caring this much about Violet Fortune was only going to hurt him—her life was in flux. But he couldn't seem to help himself.

Spotting Mrs. Gunthry, he hurried toward the table where she was sitting. When she saw him she stood, gathering her papers and file folder. "Dr. Clark. Great. I just got a call and I have to be somewhere else. But I have a few minutes."

"You said this was in regard to Celeste?"

"Yes, it is. I need you to do a complete examination, give me your treatment plan and some kind of time line for when she'll be released from here."

Peter pinned her with a long look. "I can't do that at this stage. I can give her a physical exam, but as far as the time line, that depends."

Mrs. Gunthry frowned. "I don't want her great-aunt to change her mind," she said, tapping her chin.

"Great-aunt? The one who didn't want her?"

"Yes, well, we've been in discussions with her. If Celeste can walk and take care of herself, the woman will take her. Celeste *is* going to walk again, right?"

"That's my hope, but as I said, this is early in her therapy. Violet Fortune is probably having lunch with her right now. I think we should include her in this discussion."

"Oh, I've already talked to Dr. Fortune."

"What did she say?"

"She didn't say much at all."

Peter knew he had to be rational about this. "Do you have the report you wrote up on Celeste's aunt?"

"I can't give that to you."

"Yes, I think you can. As her physician, I should be able to see everything that concerns her. And this certainly concerns her. So you either tell me about the report, or you let me read it."

Apparently guessing she wasn't going to be able to leave until all of Peter's questions were answered, she took the report from her file folder and handed it to him.

As he read it, his scowl deepened. "These are exact quotes from the aunt?"

"Yes, they are," Mrs. Gunthry said, looking chagrined.

Anger rose inside of Peter, fast and hot. *I suppose it's my duty to take a relative who has nowhere to go.* And farther down the page— *She'll be in school all day. When she gets home I'll give her supper and she'll go to bed. A few years from now she'll be a big help to me.*

"Does Dr. Fortune know this woman's attitude?"

"I gave her the gist of it. She's probably just glad the little girl will have a place to go when she leaves here. That's what important, isn't it, Dr. Clark?"

"Hell, no! There are a lot of things more important than that." Disappointment in Violet stabbed him deep. He'd thought she was different from Sandra.

"Yes, well, we can talk about this further at a later date," Mrs. Gunthry stated. "But right now I have to be going. I'll be in touch, Dr. Clark."

"Not if I'm in touch with you first," he muttered, then went to look for Violet.

Celeste's room was empty. In the PT room he found her on the mat with the therapist. Better he didn't talk to her until after he'd found Violet.

Going to the parking lot, he saw Violet's car was still there, so she was somewhere around. The longer it took him to find her, the angrier he got. Finally, he spied her sitting on a low retaining wall at the rear of the building. When he approached her, he couldn't read her expression.

"I spoke with Mrs. Gunthry," he said curtly.

"So did I."

"Yes. She told me. And I can't believe you're just going to let this happen. This relative of Celeste's could care less about her. After all these weeks of bonding with her, you're just going to break away and set her adrift with a stranger. I suspected your career would be more important than she is, that your needs and goals would dictate your life, and I was right."

Violet looked stunned for a few seconds, then exploded. "You hypocrite!"

"I am not—"

"Yes, you are! Your needs and goals dictate *your* life. So why are you judging me? You have no right to assume what I'm going to do. How could you even *think* that I would let Celeste go with a stranger who doesn't want her?"

"Mrs. Gunthry said—"

"I don't care what Mrs. Gunthry said. I didn't tell her what I was going to do because I needed to think about it. Adopting a child isn't something I take lightly."

He'd seen Violet upset before, over the whole

situation with Ryan, but he'd never seen her truly angry till now. Her blue eyes seemed to flash silver sparks, and her hair swung along her chin like a war helmet. Her cheeks were spotted with color.

"You *are* going to adopt her?" he asked with a sinking sensation in his stomach.

"Yes. That's what I want. But the fact that you could even think I'd abandon her—"

Violet's voice broke and Peter could see that behind the anger was a world of hurt. He'd caused that. He'd caused that because he'd expected her to act like Sandra Mason. He'd caused that because he'd expected her to put love aside in favor of her own needs. "Violet—"

"I thought you had feelings for me. I thought you knew what kind of person I was. But if you jumped to the wrong conclusion so readily, then you don't know me at all. And I wonder how much you feel. All this talk about jobs and different cities. You want what's convenient for you. Well, apparently *I'm* not. Go back to your practice and your life, Peter. I'm going to spend some time with Celeste, have lunch with her, tell her how much I love her, and then I'm going to contact Mrs. Gunthry and declare my intention to adopt her. I won't give Celeste up to a woman who doesn't care—not without a fight."

Before he could even think about apologizing, before he could decide how much she'd said was true, she stormed away from him and disappeared into the rehab building.

He considered going after her, but he didn't know what he would say. When he spoke to Violet again, he was going to have to do more than apologize—he was going to have to tell her what was in his heart.

He had to make damn sure the words came out right.

Jason Wilkes was sitting at his massive walnut desk at Fortune TX, Ltd. Monday afternoon crunching numbers on the computer when the commotion began. He heard a noise in the hall. Voices. A shout.

Pushing away from his desk, he rose from the burgundy leather high-backed chair, buttoned his suit coat, went to the door and looked out. Ryan Fortune was standing in the corridor, a crowd gathering around him. A woman with a cassette recorder was firing questions at him.

Jason hadn't even known Ryan was in the building. He always made a point of sucking up to the old man whenever he could. Today Ryan *looked* old. There were creases on his tanned face that hadn't been there before. Being a suspect in a murder investigation was wearing him down.

And that nicely placed article in the *Red Rock Gazette*...

Jason didn't know the woman reporter. She had red hair and long legs, and a figure that rivaled Melissa's. In her tailored tan pantsuit, she was enjoyable to watch as she levered herself in front of Ryan Fortune and wouldn't let him evade her.

"You're an influential man in this community, Mr. Fortune."

"I'm a citizen, just like everyone else. And I deserve some privacy, too."

"I think the *Red Rock Gazette* did away with your privacy. Is it true you're related to Farley Jamison, the man who was kicked out of Iowa politics because he was corrupt?"

"No comment."

"But it *is* true that your father, Kingston Fortune, was not really a Fortune?"

"He *was* a Fortune."

"Not biologically."

"When a child is adopted into a family, he or she is part of that family."

"Maybe so. But that doesn't hide the fact that his mother dropped him in Dora and Hobart Fortune's lap because she didn't want him."

Ryan remained stonily silent.

Other employees of Fortune TX, Ltd. had come to their office doors and were now staring at the whole production in the hall, too.

There was only one thing to do, Jason thought cynically. Everyone else could watch the show, but he was going to do something about it. He was going to stay in Ryan Fortune's good graces for as long as he could. The old boy looked like he needed help and Jason was going to give it.

Not waiting a second longer, he straightened his tie, then headed for the fray, addressing the reporter. "I don't know how you got past security, but you don't belong here. You have no right to accost Mr. Fortune in his own building."

"Accost? I'm just asking him a few questions."

Placing a hand on Ryan's shoulder, Jason nudged him toward his own office. "Mr. Fortune isn't answering any of your questions." He took out his cell phone. "I can call security and have a guard remove you or you can leave of your own accord. Which is it going to be?"

The reporter looked none too happy.

"What's your name?" she asked quickly.

"My name is Jason Wilkes. Now what's it going to be?"

"I'll leave," she said with a little shrug. "But don't think this is over. Anything about the Fortune family is big news."

Turning his back on her, Jason walked with Ryan down the hall.

When they were both inside his office, Jason closed the door and locked it. "It might be better if you wait here for a few moments, just to make sure she didn't bring anybody else with her."

"That's probably a good idea," Ryan said with a sigh, sinking down into a leather chair in front of Jason's desk. He took off his Stetson and set it on his knee. "Thanks for that. I appreciate it."

"No problem. Do we have an unguarded back entrance where she might have slipped in?" He was one of the team, and he wanted Ryan to know that.

"I don't know. I'll have security check all of the entrances." Ryan rubbed his temple.

"You look beat. Are you feeling okay?" Jason wasn't sure what made him ask, but he usually followed where his instincts led.

Ryan's eyes were steady as he lowered his hand and responded, "I'm fine. Just tired. I had a trip a few days ago. I'm not as young as I used to be," he added with a smile. Then as if he remembered something, he said, "One of the VP's told me you were here most of the weekend. Don't you know you need downtime, too?"

"There's still work to do, even on weekends," Jason answered with a good-old-boy smile.

"I wish some of the other employees were as dedicated as you are." Then Ryan frowned. "On the other hand, if they were, they'd probably all be divorced and their kids would grow up without them knowing them. I don't imagine your wife likes all the hours you put in."

Jason couldn't help himself from looking for something snide in that remark. He also looked for the desire Ryan might feel toward Melissa. After all, she was a beautiful woman who was playing up to him. But he didn't hear anything snide, nor did he read an undertone.

"We're a modern couple," Jason said easily. "We each have our own interests. I'll make it a short day and we'll do something fun tonight. Maybe we'll drive to Austin for dinner and dancing."

"Sounds like a plan." Ryan stood, went to the door and unlocked it.

"Are you sure you should go out there so soon?" Jason asked.

"I'll take my chances. I'm headed to my office. No one will bother me there. They know better. Thanks again for your help. I won't forget it."

Without a doubt, Jason knew Ryan wouldn't forget what he saw as a kindness. Ryan was that sort of man. But it hadn't been kindness that motivated Jason. His rescue of Ryan had been part of the plan—his plan to ruin Ryan Fortune.

Although Peter sat through a meeting at the hospital and then returned to Red Rock to see patients until 6:00 p.m., he was functioning on two levels. In every spare moment, in lulls in the conversation, between dictation into a tape recorder and reading patients' intake sheets before he conversed with them, Peter replayed what had happened with Violet. She'd called him a hypocrite. Maybe he was.

After Sandra Mason had aborted their child to further her career, Peter had looked at women in a different way. Any woman who was immersed in a professional life had been eliminated from his dating pool. Not only had he grieved for the child he'd never hold, but he'd vowed no woman would hurt him like that again. He'd vowed any woman he became involved with would cherish life as much as he did. Somehow, though, he'd rationalized that for a woman to cherish life, she had to put a husband and children first.

When he'd finished with the last patient on his schedule, he went to his car, knowing whom he had to see. A half hour later, he parked in front of the house that Charlene wanted to name Haven. In the past week, his dad had been helping her get it ready as they unpacked donations, filled cupboards, brought in furniture. To Peter's relief, he spotted Charlene's car in front of the house but not his father's. He needed to talk to her privately.

As he opened the door and stepped inside, he saw Charlene stacking videotapes on a shelf under the TV. Over her shoulder, she said, "I thought you were going to change the oil in Linda's car tonight. Did she decide she'd rather take it to the garage?"

"It's not Dad. It's me."

Charlene glanced over her shoulder then, and when she saw him, she sat back on her haunches. "Peter. I didn't expect to see you here tonight."

There were a couple of reasons why he had come, but they were hard to put into words. "Are you busy, or can we talk?"

"I'm busy, but not too busy that I can't talk. What can I do for you?"

Taking off his suit jacket, he tossed it over the back of the striped sofa. Then he loosened his tie. "We haven't spoken since you told me about your daughter."

Obviously surprised, Charlene sat on the floor by the videotapes with her legs crossed in front of her. "That's not unusual. The two of us not talking, I mean."

"I never gave you a chance," he said honestly, lowering himself onto the sofa.

She knew exactly what he meant. "You didn't want a new mother. You wanted to keep Estelle alive in your heart. You thought you couldn't do that and accept me, too."

"Why didn't you become bitter? Why didn't you cut me loose and forget about trying to form a relationship?"

"Because I love George, and you're his son. You're a part of him. I couldn't ignore you or forget about you. Besides, don't you know a mother never stops trying?"

Her words tightened his chest. "So you worried like a mother, even though I didn't want you there?"

"I worried, and prayed, and wondered if I'd lose you, like I lost my first child."

"But now you have her back?"

"I don't know. It's probably too soon to tell. But she's open to a friendship with me, and that's a start."

"Is it too late for us to be friends?"

She turned the tables on him. "What do you think?"

"I think, if I were you, I'd call me a few names and tell me to hit the road."

"But I'm not you. And you know what, Peter? I don't think that's what you'd do, either. In spite of not letting me into your life, you've turned into a decent guy."

There was amusement in her eyes, and he had to smile back. But then he thought about Violet. "Maybe not so decent."

"What happened?"

After he raked his hand through his hair, he shook his head. "I blew everything with Violet."

"Define 'blew.'"

"We got close. But the closer we got, the more turmoil she was in. My practice is here and hers is in New York. Not only that, she was considering adopting Celeste."

"And?"

"And I put two and two together and got

five." He explained what happened at the rehab center.

"Your father told me what happened between you and Sandra Mason."

The only person Peter had confided in had been his dad. "He tells you everything, doesn't he?"

"I hope so. That's what marriage is about—two people sharing everything."

Thinking about that for a few moments, he finally admitted, "I let the past shadow the future. I thought the worst when I should have thought the best."

"Exactly what do you feel for Violet?" his stepmother asked.

"I love her." There was no hesitation and he didn't even have to think about it.

"Does she know that?" Charlene's eyes were concerned, as if she already knew the answer.

"I doubt it. *I* didn't realize it until this afternoon when she stormed away. I thought about what my life would be like if she shut me out, if she went back to New York with Celeste and decided she didn't need me in her life. I don't want to lose her. I can't lose her."

Rising to her feet now, Charlene came around the coffee table and sat beside him on the sofa. "You know, don't you, that no woman is perfect, just as no man is perfect. But if two people are willing to compromise, they can be perfect for each other."

Why hadn't he ever seen Charlene's wisdom before?

Because he hadn't wanted to see it, just as he hadn't wanted to see his love for Violet. Love made a man vulnerable. After Sandra, he'd vowed never to be vulnerable again. At least that was what he'd decided with his head. His heart had had other ideas, especially where Violet was concerned.

"I love her just the way she is," he assured Charlene. "Now it might be too late. I don't think she's even going to want to talk to me. I hurt her by judging her. I hurt her by jumping to conclusions that were rooted in my fears. How's she going to forgive that?"

"Lots of women have a tremendous capacity for forgiveness, Peter. If you're honest and sincere, if you show her you're not going to give up, she'll talk to you."

"Can I have that in writing?" he asked wryly.

"You don't need it in writing. You just need the courage to tell the woman you love how much you love her."

Turning to Charlene, he said with heartfelt sincerity, "Thank you." Then awkwardly, he gave her a hug. She mustn't have felt the awkwardness because she hugged him back tightly.

When she leaned away, her eyes were filled with tears. "I've waited for this moment for a very long time."

"I'm glad my dad found you."

"I'm glad I found your dad." She brushed away her tears. "Now you go tell Violet what you need to tell her."

Peter had a stop to make before he drove to the Flying Aces. If Violet needed to see that he wouldn't give up, he needed something tangible to convince her.

Chapter 14

"Are you sure about this?" Lacey asked Violet, her voice filled with motherly worry. "Do you need me to come to Red Rock?"

"No, I'm fine, Mom." Violet didn't want to cut short her parents' New Orleans trip. She hated even calling her mother there, but some things couldn't wait. "And to answer your first question, I'm sure. I spoke with Celeste's social worker this afternoon. She called Celeste's great-aunt and it seems the woman was rationalizing to make the situation work. But when presented with the needs of a six-year-old, a six-year-old who is still recuperating, she realized she wasn't up to taking care of her. I think she felt bound by duty, and my offer to adopt Celeste released her from that."

"If you move to Red Rock, you'll have to apply for your license in Texas."

"I know that. I'm not sure how soon I'll want to start practicing here, and that's what I wanted to talk to you about. I know how much you like me being a doctor, seeing my name in medical journals. But I feel... I feel being a mother to Celeste is just as important."

"Oh, honey. I'm proud of you no matter what you do. If you want to sell hot dogs on a street corner, that's fine with me as long as you're happy."

With her mother's words, Violet felt as if a great burden had been lifted from her shoulders. She'd become a doctor, in part, because of her mother—her encouragement, her enthusiasm, her reach-for-the-stars attitude. Not that she didn't enjoy her profession. "I don't think I'll be selling hot dogs on the corner, but I do think I'll practice medicine part-time until Celeste gets older."

"Do you really think she'll recover completely?"

"The signs are good. But if she doesn't, my life plan is going to be flexible."

"Can you tell me why you don't want to bring

her back to New York? I mean, you're already established there. *We're* there. I could help you with her."

"That's a wonderful idea, Mom, and I want you to spend lots of time with her. But I need to stay in Red Rock."

"This doesn't have anything to do with your brothers, does it?"

"No."

Her heart ached when she thought of Peter and tears burned in her eyes. He'd been so willing to think the worst of her. Yet she wondered if that was her own fault because she'd been indecisive. She hadn't known which road to take. She hadn't realized exactly how important he was to her. They had something special if she hadn't destroyed it by the way she'd spoken to him, by the way *she'd* judged *him,* calling him a hypocrite. That hadn't been her brightest move. But no matter, she loved him. It was as simple and as complicated as that.

If she stayed in Red Rock, maybe he'd see she was willing to change her life, not only for Celeste, but for him, too. "I'm staying for lots of reasons," she told her mother.

"Peter Clark."

"Am I so transparent? You only saw us together for about two minutes."

"Two minutes was all it took. I heard Miles and Clyde are taking bets on whether you'll go back to New York."

"Remind me to wring their necks."

Her mother laughed. "They love you, just as we all love you."

"I didn't mean to intrude into your vacation."

"My children don't intrude. Not ever."

"What are you and Dad doing tonight?"

"Going to a blues club."

"I'm going to miss you both."

"Your dad's been cutting back his hours. We'll visit you a lot. And who knows? When he retires, maybe we'll end up in Red Rock, too. All of our children will be there. Why would we want to stay in New York? Besides, with you having Celeste and your brothers having my grandchildren in the near future—except for Miles, of course, who will probably remain a bachelor until his dying day—I'll want to be in Red Rock. I hear grandchildren keep a woman young."

Violet was sure Lacey Fortune would always be young at heart. "I'll let you go and get dressed now."

"And what are you going to do? Make lists?"

Her mother knew her so well. "How did you guess? I have to find an apartment for me and

Celeste. The pool house just isn't big enough. And then I want to decorate her room with everything a little girl should have. I have to investigate the schools in the area and—"

Lacey laughed. "Don't try to do it all in one day."

"I won't." She paused. "Thanks for understanding, Mom."

"There wasn't much to understand. I always knew you were meant to be a mother. I didn't expect it to happen in just this way, but that's what's so wonderful about life, a new surprise around every corner."

"Tell Dad I love him and give him a kiss for me."

"Will do. Keep in touch. We'll be back in New York in a few days."

After Violet hung up the phone, she felt at loose ends. She thought about calling Peter and at least leaving the message she'd be staying in Red Rock. It would warn him she wasn't going to give up on them. But he still might believe they weren't suited to each other. Somehow, she had to show him they could both meld their lives and find the happiness they were looking for.

On the other hand, if he couldn't trust her love…

The sound of tires on the gravel outside told her she had company. Or maybe Clyde and Jessica had company. When Clyde wasn't working, the couple was still definitely on their honeymoon. She'd seen Jessica pulling Clyde into the barn one afternoon, and she'd suspected what that was all about. She and Peter had almost—

There was a loud knock on her French door, and she realized she was holding her breath. When she opened it, Peter stood there, looking so serious she wanted to cry. She had a feeling he'd come to tell her they weren't right for each other, that there was no point in continuing their relationship. They were too different, too—

"Can I come in?"

Her mind had been racing so fast, she had to mentally stop it. Backing up a few steps, she said, "Sure."

She was still wearing the clothes she had dressed in that morning—jeans and a western-cut blouse. She felt as if she'd been through a war and wished she'd taken time to freshen up. But how she looked probably had nothing to do with what Peter had to say.

The awkwardness between them was only overshadowed by the intense attraction she still felt toward him. But now she didn't know if he felt it, too. There was no indication that he did. His stance was rigid, his demeanor sober, his green eyes dark. She wished he'd just blurt out what he had to say.

He did. "I was wrong this afternoon."

"Peter—"

Holding up his hand, he ordered, "Let me finish."

She fell silent and waited, her heart racing, her hands sweating.

"Over the past couple of years, and maybe even before that, I've erected walls to keep love out. I first did it with Charlene. I didn't want her taking my mother's place, and I was determined nobody would. End of story. I couldn't seem to connect with women I dated because I wouldn't *let* myself connect. Maybe wanting to have a family and settle down pushed me toward Sandra. I don't know. Maybe it was pure lust. But when she aborted our child to pursue her career, something in me died. Or at least I thought it had. Until I met you."

Now he brushed his thumb along her cheekbone and she trembled from his touch. "Somehow you got behind those walls, and you invaded my heart. I've been fighting my feelings for you as hard as I can. When we were in New York City, I felt way too vulnerable. That's not a state I've been in very often. I expected our involvement to end. I was sure it would. After all, you have a career like Sandra's, and you have every right to go back to it, if that's what you want."

His hand slipped to his side, but he went on quickly, "This afternoon I had no right to judge you or make an assumption about you or even think I had any right to say what I thought you should do. But whether you adopt Celeste or not, whether you go back to New York or don't, I want you to know how much I love you."

Deafening silence filled the room as she stared at him, stunned. Finally, she found the words she had to say. "I'm not the homebody you want," she protested feebly, wanting him to make sure he knew what he wanted because there were some things she might not be able to change.

With a gentle smile, he assured her, "I don't care about a homebody. I want *you.* I'll even move to New York if that's where you want to live. We could set up a practice together and complement each other."

Slipping a box from his trousers pocket, he handed it to her. "This wasn't what I expected to buy when I went into the jewelry store. I wanted to buy you an engagement ring so fantastic you couldn't even think about saying no. But then I realized a big diamond wouldn't do it. Besides, you're the type of woman who might want to pick out her own engagement ring. So instead, I got you this."

Feeling as if she were floating in a dream, Violet took the small box, removed the white bow and then the blue paper. She set the wrappings aside and lifted the lid. In the box, on a bed of cotton, were two halves of a solid gold heart. One half hung on a very delicate gold chain. The other half dangled from a masculine-looking chain.

Removing the necklaces, Peter tossed the box aside. Taking her hand, he placed one half of the heart in her palm. "We can wear these until you pick out an engagement ring. Half is yours and half is mine. If you marry me, we can be whole together."

Tears flooded her eyes and ran down her cheeks. "Oh, Peter."

He was looking worried. "Is that a good 'Oh, Peter,' or a get-out-of-my-life 'Oh, Peter'?"

When she handed him back the necklace, she saw the desolation on his face until she said, "Will you put it on me?"

She saw him swallow hard. Then he turned her around and attached the necklace. By the time she faced him again, he was wearing the other half.

Unable to contain her joy, she threw her arms around his neck. "I was so hoping you wouldn't be mad at me forever."

"Mad at you? For telling me the truth? I hope we can always tell each other the truth."

"Always," she agreed, right before his mouth claimed hers.

The kiss went on and on and on until he swung her up into his arms and carried her to the bed. But as they lay together, he didn't undress her and she didn't undress him. They gazed into each other's eyes, holding each other, getting used to the idea that they didn't have to be separated again.

"I can't believe you'd decided you'd move to New York," she said in awe. "That isn't what I want. I want to stay here, in Red Rock. But I am going to adopt Celeste." She leaned away slightly. "Are you okay with that?"

"Okay? Bringing you two together was my idea in the first place. I love that little girl. I want to give her a home and a place to belong. If we get married right away, we'll have time for our honeymoon before we start really being parents."

"When do you think she'll be ready to come home?"

"Maybe two months," he admitted. "But as soon as possible, we'll get her switched to outpatient therapy. Whatever happens, we'll deal with it together. That's what marriage is all about."

With a frown he said, "I don't think you answered my question."

"And that question was?" she teased.

"Will you marry me?"

"In a New York minute," she breathed, her hands going to the buttons of his shirt, her lips trailing kisses along his jawline.

"I'm not sure I know the difference between a New York minute and a Texas minute. But I do know loving you for a lifetime won't be nearly enough."

"Oh, Peter."

This time he obviously knew happiness threaded her words because he kissed her long and hard and deep. Then he made love to her, showing her exactly how wonderful their future would be.

Epilogue

On Tuesday Violet went along with Peter and waited as he made rounds at the hospital. Then they went to Tumbleweed Terrace Rehab Hospital to have a special lunch with Celeste. They took along with them pictures of Peter's house, and all the joy in their hearts.

When they arrived, Celeste was sitting in a wheelchair by the window in her room, waiting for lunch. "I got a roommate," she told them happily when she saw them. "Her name's Cindy. She has to use a wheelchair, too. Her mommy and daddy wheeled her outside."

At the mention of a mommy and daddy Violet glimpsed a sadness that was ever-present in Celeste's eyes. Pulling a chair next to Celeste, she sat and took the child's hand in hers. She glanced up at Peter, and at his nod, she smiled at the little girl who was going to be her daughter. "Peter and I have something we want to tell you."

"What?" She looked almost scared.

"We're going to get married."

"And you're going to live together?"

"Yep, that's part of it," Peter said with a chuckle. "But it's a lot more than that, too. We're going to love each other for always and always."

"And," Violet continued, "we want you to be our little girl."

Celeste was silent for a very long time.

Trying to keep the worry from her voice, Violet asked, "What do you think about that?"

"Will I come live with you?"

"As soon as you're well enough to leave here," Peter assured her.

After she considered that, she asked, "And you won't give me away? Ever?"

"Not ever," Violet promised her, her voice tight.

"And you won't leave me all by myself?"

"We will *never* leave you all by yourself. Not

until you're old enough to want to be by yourself," Peter vowed.

"When I'm ten?" she asked, intrigued.

"Maybe when you're sixteen," Peter muttered, and Violet had to laugh.

Again, silence fell in the room, and Violet couldn't take it. "Do you have any more questions?"

Celeste's dark eyes got very big and her chin quivered a little when she asked, "Can I call you Mommy and Daddy?"

Unable to get any words out, Violet was filled with happiness. Peter stepped behind her and put one arm around Celeste and one arm around his wife-to-be. "You bet you can call us Mommy and Daddy."

Celeste's face broke into a wide grin and sunshine seemed to fill the room. "Then I want to be your little girl."

Whether it was official or not, Violet already thought of Celeste as her daughter. Squeezing Celeste's hand, she looked up at her husband-to-be. As he kissed her temple and held her tight, she knew they'd found their future. Their love would be the beginning. Each day they'd be thankful for what they'd found.

She fingered the half of the heart that lay

against her sweater. They were soul mates, friends, lovers, doctors and partners. She'd found the perfect man to make happily ever after a reality rather than a dream.

* * * * *